TRIDENT

by John Passmore

SAMSARA PRESS

Book cover design by www.BeyondBookCovers.com

© John Passmore 2017 All rights reserved

ONE

The little lies are the hardest.

There was a space on the man's passport for "Distinguishing Marks". The space was empty – yet beneath the fawn anorak he carried over his arm there was no third finger on his left hand. It was an old injury which he normally ignored. But now it throbbed as if crying out to be noticed. It always did going through passport control.

If anyone asked, he would say there had been an accident in his uncle's workshop when he was a boy and that if he mentioned it everyone would want to see. Neither explanation was the truth – but then, he was never asked. He just felt awkward.

The Special Branch man who stood beside the passport desk saw only what the passport described – a 34-year-old Belgian engineer, one Marcel Redon, wearing a sweater and carrying a holdall and with a big sombre face that did not match anything on the terrorist files.

The passport clerk looked at the face, the Special Branch man looked at the face and the man with no third finger on his left hand, who called himself Marcel Redon, stared back. Then he stepped safely into England.

He sat on the subway train which the British call "The Tube" and read his English newspaper. It was full of election news. He had never taken much interest in British politics. He knew, he supposed, as much as any other intelligent stranger to the country – and he knew about the

Peace Movement.

The Peace Movement had only one item on its manifesto: Total and unilateral nuclear disarmament. It made no pretence at having an economic policy or suggesting what might be done with the health service. Since its supporters had come from all parties in roughly equal numbers, they would never agree anyway. But they did make the prospect of disarmament more real than it had ever been before.

The train started and the man who called himself Marcel Redon turned to the cartoon. It showed a map of Europe. There were nuclear disarmament flags on France, Germany, Holland - all the countries which no longer had nuclear weapons on their soil. And in Britain Malcolm Japp, the benign, white-haired leader of the Peace Movement was busily sweeping a pile of missiles into the sea - unaware that behind him President Narbokov was reaching out from a Soviet Union filled to bursting point with missiles and gleefully pinning a flag on Mr Japp's backside.

The man who called himself Redon turned the page. He glanced at the previews of the football matches which by now had been played and noted that l00,000 people were expected at Sunday's Peace Movement rally in Trafalgar Square. Then he folded the paper and sat quietly until the train reached Knightsbridge.

He walked westwards and went into Harrods. The store was packed with Saturday shoppers and he pushed his way quickly the entire length of the ground floor. He caused a great deal of nuisance - but anybody following him would have been equally conspicuous. By the time he emerged in the menswear department and went into the tunnel to the multi-storey car park. he knew he was alone.

The car was a typically anonymous family saloon, parked just where he had been told it would be on the second floor. He walked past, checking the others but there was no-one watching it - only a middle-aged couple loading shopping bags into a Mercedes. He waited for them to go.

He went back to the car, took a key from his pocket and opened the boot. He pulled out a brown canvas holdall, replaced it with the identical one from his shoulder, slammed the boot shut and was on his way before anyone else appeared.

The new bag was much heavier than the old but he hooked it casually over his shoulder and went out into the street. Harrods was closing and he was in a crowd again. He smiled. He felt safe.

The first marchers entered the square at noon. They carried a banner half the width of the road bearing the words "Vote for Peace". Several photographers walked backwards as they took pictures of Malcolm Japp against a background of his followers.

High above them and a kilometre to the east, in the cabin of a bright yellow crane, the man who called himself Marcel Redon took a pair of binoculars from his holdall and looked down. The familiar rubbery face leapt back at him, magnified eight times. It was a face people trusted - a kindly face with twinkling blue eyes and framed in a halo of wispy white hair. Malcolm Japp's face had become the symbol of the Peace Movement.

He was an ordinary man, not an extremist - and that was why ordinary people had begun to follow him. They had seen what had happened in the rest of Europe: They had watched the socialist government of West Germany rescue its economy almost overnight by voting to pull out of NATO. They had listened to a blustering American president threaten to refuse help in the event of a Soviet attack - and they had delighted in the cocky little Herr Gruber explaining that he had no intention of allowing foreign armies to fight their wars in his country.

It was, of course, the beginning of the end of NATO. In the space of six years every European member of the alliance had followed Germany - and since this did not provoke an immediate Soviet invasion, it was followed in turn by a wave of sympathy for the anti-nuclear lobby. The French government had already bowed to the pressure and abolished its *force de frappe* - and now the issue had taken over the British election and prompted a new man in the White House to warn pompously, "If you lay aside your shield, we will not protect you."

But the voters were reminded by the homely and reasonable Malcolm Japp that the Trident submarine programme had finally cost three times its original estimate. They were invited to compare Britain's six million unemployed with the Germans' one million.

So why wasn't the Peace Movement about to win the General Election? The political commentators knew, Malcolm Japp probably knew, deep down - and the man in the crane certainly knew.

The Peace Movement was not going to win because there were still too many people in Britain who had learned from their parents and grandparents what happened in 1939. It would take another five or even ten years of Germany living peacefully cheek by jowl with communism before that stubborn British pride would subside - and even five years was going to be too long.

As Malcolm Japp scraped a hand through his hair and mounted the rostrum, the man in the crane opened his holdall and began to assemble his rifle. The weapon was ideally suited for this kind of work: A British Army issue Heckler and Koch GII carrying 108 rounds of 4.7mm caseless ammunition. Because there were no cartridge cases to be ejected and the square firing charges evaporated completely, the rifle was capable of firing at any rate between single shots and 2,000 rounds a minute. At that setting the bullets emerged from the muzzle in a constant stream, nose to tail.

The crowd had fallen silent, only a few good-natured shouts reached the crane. The man who called himself Redon laid his cheek against the stock and switched on the laser sight. The image flared up brightly and then settled. The sight made abrupt dull buzzing sounds as it compensated for the range, first on the buildings at the other side of the square, then the crowd and finally the figure on the rostrum. The twin dots converged just in front of the ear. The white hair quivered as the head jerked in rhetoric. This was not the time. Wait for it to be still.

The speech seemed to go on for an age. The jerking head leapt about against the dot in the centre of the sight. Suddenly it stopped. Half a second later the sound of cheers reached the crane in a long, rumbling sigh. The head remained steady.

The man behind the rifle took a slow breath, moved the dot a fraction to the left and squeezed the trigger.

The head, like a target in a fairground shooting gallery disappeared abruptly. In fact it disintegrated, unable to absorb some 15 bullets delivered in the half-second burst. But the assassin did not look to see what had happened to his target. Even as the short scream of the gun echoed back from the surrounding buildings, he was laying it aside and throwing a length of black polyester rope out of the door of the cabin. It took him no more than five seconds to abseil to the ground. Within two minutes he was walking briskly towards the square. The people came running. People shocked and frightened, some in tears. He asked them what was happening and the reports were confused. It was not long before he was swallowed up in a crowd of several thousand, anonymous, safe...

He sat in the departure lounge of Manchester Airport. He wore a dark grey suit and his passport said his name was

Josef Muller. aged 36, a salesman from Frankfurt. The passport made no mention of distinguishing marks but Herr Muller kept his left hand covered by his raincoat.

It would have seemed odd if he had not been watching the television. At least half of the monitor screens had been switched from flight information to the news. Passengers and airport staff stood and watched the report of the assassination of Malcolm Japp four hours earlier. Apparently, the murder weapon, a high powered rifle, had been found but as yet no other details were available and so far no group had claimed responsibility.

In the absence of any other information, the presenter introduced once more that dramatic piece of film: Japp was standing motionless on the rostrum with his arms outstretched as the crowd roared its approval. Suddenly he seemed to be propelled sideways. The film slowed now as the old man fell against one of his aides, his whole head a red blur. The other man crumpled too, falling over on top of Japp, one arm flailing and knocking the microphone to the ground.

Now the people behind them registered surprise while others stood smiling and clapping, gazing out beyond the camera. The two bodies were now below the level of the banner across the front of the rostrum. The first people to react were moving towards them, hands outstretched. The film stopped then and the presenter read the latest bulletin on the second man shot in the attack, a member of the Peace Movement's national executive who was seriously injured and undergoing an emergency operation at the Westminster Hospital.

And now, some of the tributes which had been pouring in for Malcolm Japp: The leaders of the other parties spoke of the loss to democracy. His archrival of the Conservatives explained how, while he might not have agreed with Malcolm Japp on matters of policy, he nevertheless respected him as a man of the highest ideals.

Mr Japp's widow Maureen, seen at the door of her North London home, looked drawn but composed. She read a short statement: "Malcolm devoted his life to the cause of peace. Now he has died for it. If this terrible tragedy is to have any meaning at all, let us pray that through his death, he may help to bring to fruition the dream for which he worked so long."

A statement issued by Buckingham Palace said that the King and Queen had sent a private message of sympathy to Mr Japp's family.

There followed a discussion with the BBC's political correspondent about the direction the Peace Movement would take now and who would lead it in the election only four days away.

The political correspondent felt the tragedy was bound to create enormous public sympathy for the Movement but it did once again open up the whole issue of a referendum on unilateral disarmament. This, of course, had never been satisfactorily resolved in conference and only Malcolm Japp's perseverance had kept the party together. Now everything depended on who would take over the leadership - and that was something which had to be decided as soon as possible.

The screen reverted to showing flight information and at the same time the public-address system announced that Lufthansa flight LH 075 to Frankfurt was now boarding. The man who called himself Josef Muller picked up his briefcase and moved towards the gate.

TWO

If the committee had known about Bernie Price, they would never have let him in.

But then Bernie Price did not look like a newspaper reporter. He was a dapper little man who owned three suits in different shades of green tweed and three trilby hats to match. He always had clean fingernails, called all sorts of people "Sir" and had a twinkle in his eye.

And considering the nearest he had come to a military career had been the Sea Scouts, he was remarkably well-accepted in the Army and Navy Club.

He lunched there about once a month with a Major Jeremy Johnson, known as "Porky" throughout the Ministry of Defence where he ran the admin office of the intelligence department. He was, of course, still an intelligence officer, standing his turn of duty with the rest. But at 52 years old he was filling in time until his pension and everyone knew it. Nobody ever told Porky any proper secrets.

But this didn't matter to Bernie Price. Official Secrets of that sort never got into newspapers anyway. He was after the military gossip, the little titbits which anyone at the ministry might know. They were well worth the generous contribution Bernie made every month towards the cost of the lunch. Since the club menu did not include the prices, it was not surprising that he wildly over-estimated the bill.

The Major was in the bar, squirting soda into his scotch. He motioned to the steward for another and leaned forward, conspiratorially, as he grasped the newsman's hand. "Got something for you, old boy. Make your hair curl."

Bernie always felt slightly uncomfortable at this moment. Most of the Major's "Red Hot Scoops" turned out to be useless. It was his casual asides which had more than once filled the front page and led to questions in Parliament.

This time Bernie allowed himself to be steered to a corner table where the Major lost no time in announcing, "They found the gun."

"I know," said Bernie. "In the crane."

"No, they've found out where it came from. Feller had tried to file off the serial number but the forensics people have got some X-Ray or something that can read it anyway. It's one of ours. Registered at Colchester Barracks. There's a hell of a stink.

Bernie leaned closer so that he could smell the whisky on the Major's breath: "Porky, are you telling me that someone broke into the armoury at Colchester barracks and walked out with one of the most advanced and deadly assault rifles in the world?"

The Major failed to meet his eye. "Can't see how anyone could get away with that - place is locked up tight as a drum."

"Inside job, then?"

"Looks like it."

"So what we're looking at is the Army colluding in a political assassination four days before a general election? Is that right?"

"I didn't say that."

"No, you didn't. But Porky, I think you deserve another drink all the same."

The worst thing about solitary breakfasts is that you can't take your time over them. If you prop the paper against the coffee pot, put your elbows on the table and rest the lip of the cup against your chin, inhaling the sweet wet steam, then - even in a four-star Swiss hotel - the waiters will begin to noisily lay the next table for lunch.

But Elizabeth Crichton went on reading the hotel's complementary English paper. It was 24 hours old and predictably full of the progress of the new Government's disarmament policy. The writer even had a snide dig at the Peace Movement by reporting an attempt to re-christen the Ministry of Defence the "Ministry of Peace"- until someone had explained the Orwellian overtones. But while the name remained the same, everything else was changing. The new minister was someone called Vincent Earlham. Elizabeth thought she had heard of him. She ought to know more - after all, he would be her new boss.

But to a humble executive officer among a staff of 22 in the Secretary of State's private office, it didn't much matter who the minister was. She doubted he would speak to her - the last one hadn't.

She sat there feeling vaguely discontented so that it was a while before she realised there was a man standing beside her table, talking to her.

He wanted to borrow the newspaper - that was if she'd quite finished with it. He was very polite. He had short hair which made his face look rather big, but he had a nice smile. He seemed to be German. He would just skim through the paper in the lobby and give it back to her. She realised she had said nothing at all. She must seem terribly rude. "Of course. I've quite finished with it - and please keep it."

He smiled and gave a little Germanic bow and scooped up the paper.

There was something wrong about that movement. It was gruesome. The man had no third finger on his left hand, just a tiny stump of bone beneath the skin. She shivered at the thought. The poor man... She wondered what had happened to him and she carried on wondering as she went up to get changed.

She saw him again when she came down from her room in her walking boots and with her little nylon rucksack dangling from one hand. She nodded to him, politely.

He leapt to his feet - although not so quickly, she noticed, as to seem foolish. He offered her the paper.

"No really," she smiled. "I wouldn't want to spoil a day like this with the English news."

The man chuckled. "Quite right," he said. "And I must be making a start." He had a cumbersome, old fashioned rucksack on the floor beside him. The top was open and it seemed to be full of small plastic boxes.

Elizabeth became aware that she was staring at them. "You seem to be going very well prepared... "

He laughed then, a gentle uninhibited laugh: "Specimen boxes. I'm a botanist and always I am frightened that I will leave something behind."

He wasn't in fact a professional botanist - for that, as he told her, he would have to be very rich or very content with being poor. No, Lorenz Erhardt was a keen amateur who used his hobby as an antidote to the intensely practical side of his life as a structural engineer. But all the same he did know most of the flowers which grew in the mountains around Zermatt, the flowers which Elizabeth Crichton had come all the way from London to see. It was only common courtesy that he should offer to show them to her - and it was only polite of her to accept.

So together, with their rucksacks on their backs. they walked up the little town's main street to the cable car and set off up into the foothills of the Matterhorn.

*

He got her talking as they left the cable car at the Schwarzee station and set off along the path that wanders up the Hornli ridge. He had seen her picture, of course. He had memorized a selection of them when he was briefed by the sad-eyed little man from Moscow.

"Another gorgeous girl" was the way she had been described to him. She wasn't gorgeous by any means but she was an improvement on her photograph and for that he was grateful. The man who called himself Lorenz Erhardt saw no reason why life should be made unnecessarily difficult.

She seemed to have a good figure and her face was open and cheerful with a wide, full mouth and direct grey eyes. She wore her hair short. She could have dyed it something better than mouse brown - probably she couldn't be bothered. All in all, he put her down as a practical, forthright young woman who knew what she wanted. That, together with what he knew of her past, suggested she was a good choice for his purpose.

He became aware that she was talking about herself and he began to concentrate: "It's years since I took a holiday on my own." she said. "In fact I'm not sure I ever have. You know the way it is: First you go with girlfriends, then you go with boyfriends and then you're married - except of course, I wasn't actually married." She looked round at him sharply as if afraid of being thought too conventional. "My parents nagged and wittered, as parents do, but considering what happened in the end it's just as well."

"And what did happen?"

"Nothing. That's the point. Suddenly one day we discovered we had nothing to say to each other anymore. End of Romance. "

Lorenz said what he had decided he would say at this point: "I'm sorry." Out of the corner of his eye he saw her looking at him and smiling.

She said: "Anyway it's water under the bridge now. Come on, let's enjoy ourselves. Show me some flowers."

He showed her flowers. He showed her flowers by the million: tiny mauve flowers packed as thick as a mat over the pale young grass, which never had a chance between the snow one day and this wild profusion the next. He led her scrambling down the banks of a stream to see the purple Cortusa thriving in the icy spray. He marvelled with her at the endless shades of blue in the first Fairies Thimbles and of course he found her some Edelweiss.

And finally he settled down with her on the steps of a little wooden farmer's hut to eat their packed lunches of cheese and good tough dried meat and he produced a bottle of Fendant from among his collection of specimen boxes.

And she lay back and closed her eyes in the sun and he watched her and smiled a grim and satisfied smile.

*

On the first floor of Buckingham Palace, overlooking the gardens is a room called the audience chamber. The very name is enough to produce an attack of nerves in a good many of the people who call there. But on the morning after the Peace Movement won the election it was the King who stood at the window anxiously twisting the signet ring on his left hand. He was fairly certain there had never been a Prime Minister quite like the man he was about to appoint.

At 30, Michael Tattersall would not be the youngest ever British Prime Minister Britain - William Pitt still held that record - but compared to any over the last hundred years, he was a mere boy.

And not only was he young, he was idealistic, impatient and with kind of militant background which might have prepared him for leadership of one of the more extreme trade unions. The King did not believe it made him a statesman.

Most important of all, Tattersall represented that faction of the Peace Movement opposed to a referendum. The moderates who had followed Malcolm Japp had always insisted that on an issue as fundamental as this, a majority in Parliament would not be enough - only a majority of the whole electorate would stop some future government rearming.

But Malcolm Japp was gone now - and his followers were becoming increasingly angry as the details of his murder emerged. The assassin's gun had been stolen three weeks earlier from an army barracks at Colchester. The rope used in the getaway was the same kind issued to the Royal Marines and other specialist regiments. There would no longer be a single member of the Peace Movement who still believed the military would give up their nuclear weapons without a fight - and Michael Tattersall seemed very much the sort of man who would give them one.

He came in as he had been taught by the equerry: four paces, bow - four more paces. They exchanged the formal sentences and they shook hands. Then the King sat the young man down and smiled and set about putting him at his ease. He was usually very good at this - and besides, it was important. They would be meeting in this very room every Tuesday morning and as the King explained: "I am neither a politician nor a civil servant. In fact you'll probably find I'm the only person you meet without an axe to grind. I hope that will help you to trust me, because that's what I'm here for - to listen and to advise if I can."

The young man seemed surprised.

And then, with rather more difficulty than he had expected, the King raised the subject of a referendum: He quite understood that any Government with a majority in parliament was entitled to carry out its manifesto - in fact it had a duty to do so. But Malcolm Japp had said...

Tattersall began to interrupt and the King held up his hand and went on: "I know that you are now the leader and, as of this moment, the Prime Minister - but what you intend to do is so important and so irreversible that we really must be sure it's the will of the country as a whole.

"You have 37 per cent of the vote. That's not an overall majority by any means and if you go ahead with your plans and don't hold a referendum, there's going to be enormous resentment. After all a great many people were led to expect..."

This time Tattersall did interrupt. He was polite and he spoke softly but there was an intensity in his voice that did not brook argument: "With respect sir, we have the sort of majority any government might get - but it never stopped any of them carrying out their manifesto."

The King went on, logically, reasonably: "But a referendum would do no harm. If you really do have the backing of the country, then it would only reinforce your mandate. Without one there would always be disquiet. Mr Japp..."

"Malcolm Japp is dead." said the young man. "He was killed in an election campaign. Feelings are running high, perhaps that's understandable. But I don't want to risk another tragedy in a referendum campaign."

He paused, realising he was in danger of raising his voice. He went on: "Look, sir, I don't expect you to see my point of view. You're a military man. You have been all your life. Those submarines capable of bringing about the end of the world, they' re your submarines: 'His Majesty's Submarines.' Preparing for war has been your whole purpose as head of the armed forces. Obviously, you can't just shake that off. But the ordinary people of this country are different. They want peace."

The King stared at him. "You think I don't?"

But Tattersall continued: "Believe me, we're going to dismantle this so-called nuclear deterrent. It's what we promised to do. It's what we were elected to do - and now we're going to do it."

The King had known it would be like this but that didn't make it any easier. He said nothing because there seemed to be nothing useful he could say. Tattersall appeared relieved. He shook hands, gave a little nod of his head and walked quickly to the door. When the equerry entered, he found the King staring out into the garden, his hands clasped tightly behind his back.

The equerry waited a moment and then left without a word.

*

SUMMARY

Meeting of the Politburo of the Central Committee of the Communist Party of the Soviet Union. March 22nd 1999. Items 4 & 5 (Foreign Affairs), Chairman's Statement and Resolutions:

4. German Democratic Republic. Comrade the Minister for Foreign Affairs reported on the disturbances among the civil population of the German Democratic Republic (Appendix A).

Throughout the DDR there have been 1,426 arrests as a result of these disturbances. Comrade the Minister for Foreign Affairs informed the meeting that it must now be accepted that, without action by the USSR, it is likely the situation will deteriorate further for the following reasons:

i) It is expected that at their meeting on May 30th, the consortium of Western banks which has so far underwritten the national deficit will refuse to reschedule loans equivalent to 36 billion roubles.

ii) With industrial output having declined by a further nine per cent over the past six months, the hard currency trade deficit rose to 2.8 million roubles.

iii) Domestic sales of meat and cereals to the Government fell by a further two per cent over the past month. Reductions in the food ration are imminent.

In order to halt this decline, the following measures would be necessary:

i) A monthly supply of two million tonnes of grain and 1.4 million tonnes of meat and other basic foodstuffs.

ii) A guarantee to be given to the Western banks that the Soviet Union will service the DDR debts for a period of five years.

iii) Special trading status to be given to the DDR by other COMECON member states.

Failing this. Comrade the Minister for Foreign Affairs suggested that intervention by units of the Red Army would become a necessity if the security of the Warsaw Pact nations is to be maintained.

The Chairman deferred discussion on this item.

5. United Kingdom. Comrade the. Director of State Security reported that the operation to secure the election of the

Peace Movement to Government in Britain had been achieved in accordance with the resolution of February l6th (Appendix B)

As had been predicted by the KGB bureau of planning and strategy, the operation had also resulted in a high level of public anger directed against the British military elite.

Chairman's Statement: Comrade the Chairman addressed the meeting as follows (Transcript paragraphs 4l6 -428): "Two of the items we have discussed today; while seemingly diverse, are in fact closely linked in terms of a problem and its possible solution.

"On too many occasions we have sat around this table as have our predecessors - and been faced with an uprising in one of the satellites: Poland, Czechoslovakia, Hungary, even. All have fallen victim to the mischief of imperialist insurgents who use the sacrifices of the socialist peoples to spread discontent.

"And now the Democratic Republic of Germany, once the most ordered of all, is consumed with strikes and street riots.

"So, what are we to do? You have heard from Comrade the Minister for Foreign Affairs. Do we divert food from our own already overstretched resources to feed a people who seem only intent on destroying themselves? Or do we turn to the Red Army as we have so many times in the past and will again, doubtless, in the future?

"For make no mistake, this will not be the last time. The young hooligans who daub anti-state slogans on the walls of the University of Prague were not born in 1968; the pamphleteers of Warsaw are too young to remember their own sharp lesson in 1981.

"Those times will come again and one day it will not be in just one country but all the satellites simultaneously. These malcontents know the strength of numbers and ultimately, they will use it. Then we will not be faced merely with a small uprising to be put down with a handful of resolutions made here in this room. We will be faced with civil war within our own borders –a war in which we will not be able to rule out the possibility that the armies of the other Warsaw Pact nations would turn against us.

"So we must accept the possibility that if we go on as we are, we will be engaged in a war within the next ten or fifteen years - a war to maintain the status quo. It would cost us dearly and bring us nothing more than we have already.

"Now consider this: The discontent in the satellites would melt away if we had access to the food stores of Western Europe, yet it is offered to us by the West at prices we can only afford by cutting our spending on security.

"If war is to be inevitable, is that not a better reason for fighting it, with the nations of the Warsaw Pact marching shoulder to shoulder against a common enemy and towards a goal not only of feeding our hungry people but also one which would advance the cause of Marxist-

Leninism by the greatest strides in living memory.

"And for the first time we can be certain of the outcome. With the new British Government now dismantling the last nuclear weapons in Western Europe, our forces would be unstoppable.

"There are imponderables: For instance, can we be assured the British nuclear weapons could not be brought back into service? We must be certain before any move is made. But if, after careful consideration, it transpires that the time is indeed right, then we have an opportunity which we should not ignore."

RESOLUTIONS

The resolutions were carried unanimously that:

i) Provisional plans be made for a conventional strike into Western Europe.

ii) Further provisional plans be made by all departments for the support of such action.

iii) The Department of State Security will monitor the destruction of the British nuclear weapons.

iv) Preliminary arrangements be made for the guarantee of DDR loans.

v) Supplies of food and other basic commodities adequate to maintaining rations at their present level be made available to the Government of the DDR.

vi) Full discussion be deferred pending reports from all departments.

THREE

The King was sitting in his private drawing room with a cup of coffee at his side and his correspondence all over his lap.

The Queen sat in the armchair opposite, reading a charity report. She had her feet tucked up under her and looked very young indeed.

The King did not look young – and now that he was worried, he looked greyer and more tired than usual. Finally he said: "Good Lord."

The Queen looked up and found that her husband. with his usual irritating habit, continued to read to the end of the letter. Finally she said: "Good Lord, what?"

"Hmm?"

"What's so special about that letter."

"Oh, nothing really - Charles Lomas wants to resign his commission. "

She looked blank.

"You know him. Vice Admiral Sir Charles Lomas. He comes to dinner at Windsor sometimes. He's got that little Queen Anne house. "

The "little Queen Anne house", Beech Lodge, on the edge of the Royal Estate at Windsor Great Park, was something the King had arranged personally under the old custom of granting Grace and Favour homes to Royal servants of long standing.

Of course, Sir Charles was not exactly a Royal Servant,

but he had - many years before - been a great friend and advisor when the young Prince was taking his first command in the Royal Navy. When Lady Lomas had died and he talked of moving, the King had let him have the house on impulse. He always felt it was so right for an old sailor home from the sea.

And that was the most disturbing thing about the whole letter. The King went on: "He's resigning because he doesn't approve of the Government. Says he won't be associated with a service which is about to "have its teeth drawn". That's just the sort of thing he would say. I suppose we'll get a lot of this - a bit like people sending back their medals when they don't approve of some pop singer who gets one. Says he's leaving the house too."

The Queen latched onto that: "Oh no, darling, you can't l.et him do that. I mean where else can he go? And, besides, isn't he quite besotted with that little house?"

The King raised an eyebrow: Vice Admirals on index-linked pensions were quite capable of finding somewhere else to go - but that wasn't the point.

"Well, of course he can't go. The whole thing's ridiculous - quite typical of the old boy, though. He always did have an overdeveloped sense of responsibility. I'll send a note, see if I can't make him see reason. I don't understand why he's bothering to resign in the first place - it's not as if he's going to persuade our friend Tattersall to change his mind."

The Queen thought for a minute, the report now forgotten on her lap: "His son," she said. "I'll bet it's all got something to do with his son. He's Captain of one of the Trident submarines, isn't he? If they scrap them, he'll lose his ship, surely. "

The King nodded and began to make a note on the top of the letter. He said, "Boat. Submarines are called boats. Anyway, we can't have the old boy losing his house over it."

*

She loved the dress dearly. It was plain black silk and cut in that particular and expensive way that made it appear chic, while at the same time blatantly accentuating her bust and bottom. Elizabeth Crichton had never paid as much for a dress before or since - and this was the night to wear it.

Lorenz, she had discovered, was correct and polite and so exasperatingly reserved that something had to be done. For three days they had walked in the mountains and danced in the bierkellers - and each evening he had given her a courteous little bow and wished her goodnight.

If he really had been German perhaps she would have been fighting him off. But he was Swiss and shy and really rather sweet.

Whether it was the dress of whether things would have turned out the way they did without her help, she never knew. But that night everything was easy and relaxed and fun and different.

They fed each other fondue with much giggling and

danced very close together and not at all energetically. They drank moderately and as the evening calmed down, Elizabeth's head began to lie naturally on Lorenz's shoulder. By the time they left the nightclub it seemed perfectly natural to walk slowly back to the hotel with their arms twined around each other, saying nothing and looking at several million stars.

And they said nothing when he picked up both their keys at the desk and led her to her room and, still with that slightly quizzical smile, he kicked the door closed behind them and kissed her.

Elizabeth felt his hands at her back, pressing her to him, she felt the passion in him and answered with her own. She stood there, her head thrown back, his lips at her neck as, deliciously, she sensed his hands against the skin of her back and the lovely dress falling with a brief rustle around her feet. He picked her up out of it and carried her to the bed.

She still wore her underwear and wondered vaguely if she should take it off. But Lorenz was standing there smiling down at her as if everything was planned while, unhurriedly, he unfastened first one cufflink and then the other. Then his tie.

Good God, he was doing a striptease. For an instant she felt revolted by the vanity of the man and yet what he was doing was perfectly natural. There was also a calm assurance about it that was arousing, that told her she would still be there when he was ready for her. She lay back and watched. His body was hard and muscular. One day he would be fat. But not yet.

When he came to her, she held out her arms to him as if she had been waiting all her life. In a sense she had.

There was a time, somewhere in the morning of that first night when Elizabeth lay with her head on the man's chest, twirling the fine fair hairs around her finger, when she said: "I cried, you know."

"I know."

"I actually cried. That's never happened to me before. I thought it only happened in books. Here, look." She raised her head to him and he kissed her eves tenderly, tasting the dried salt tears. She kissed him back.

"You made me cry, you wonderful Swiss man. I mean I've never had any hang-ups. I've never had any trouble, you know like women do sometimes. But I've never known anything like this. It just went on and on, again and again."

He ran a finger down the length of her spine: "It's the mountains."

"It's this mountain."

"Ouch!" But she didn't let go.

And she cried again.

*

The file on the Prime Minister's desk was 22 pages long. It was delivered in a red embossed folder marked "Secret" -

and it said precisely nothing.

The Prime Minister looked across it at his Secretary of State for Defence and said: "Vincent, you're letting them walk all over you."

Then he got up and left Vincent Earlham to bluster and make excuses and say that nuclear weapons could not simply be thrown away when they were no longer needed. Proposals had to be drawn up, timetables had to be agreed...

It was the sort of thing Earlham would say. He had the job because, now Malcolm Japp was gone, he led the middle class intellectual faction of the Peace Movement. But at heart he was still an academic - an ineffectual dreamer. What he was not, was any kind of a threat to Michael Tattersall. He went on: "The Trident submarines have been recalled. That's a start."

Clearly, he believed it. Tattersall turned and looked down on him. Quietly he said: "Those submarines can put to sea at a moment's notice. They've been recalled just to make it look as though something is being done when in fact nothing is changing at all. Go back and raise hell, Vincent. We've come a long way for this and we're not going to be beaten by a bunch of civil servants throwing paper at us."

It was a dramatic gesture, of course. It might even fire Earlham into putting a squib up the backside of his department. But as the old man strode out with a show of resolution. Tattersall knew that would not be enough.

He touched the intercom button and ordered his usual

ham roll and bottle of lager. Then he flipped open the report once more and read again the official nuclear statistics which he had always suspected but never seen confirmed before.

The whole thing was obscene: For a start, even though the Royal Air Force was no longer the primary nuclear arm, it still accounted for more than twice as many weapons as the other two services combined. In all, the Tornadoes and Jaguars could deliver 380 bombs - and that was quite apart from the 120 still held in store for the now obsolete Buccaneers.

The Army still had some 270 nuclear shells but no missiles since the American-controlled Lance system had gone back across the Atlantic with the break-up of NATO. All the same the Navy had 130 nuclear depth bombs - and, of course, the Navy had Trident.

Trident was the key. While the shells and bombs were undoubtedly appalling weapons, they were designed for battlefield use - for use against troops. The Trident system was designed to kill civilians and to kill them on a scale which the mind of a sane man could not comfortably comprehend. Michael Tattersall knew that each submarine carried 16 multiple warhead missiles together capable of destroying 224 medium-sized cities. Multiply that by four submarines and you were talking about 1,000 cities. It was that capability for mass murder which must be brought to an end first. There were only 64 missiles compared to the hundreds of shells and bombs - yet it was the missiles which captured the imagination and as long as they remained in the submarines, supposedly waiting their turn to be dismantled, they could be brought back into service at a moment's notice.

Tattersall put down the report, stood his empty glass on top of it and considered his options. It did not take him long to decide to start at the top. He leaned forward to his intercom and said: "Make an appointment for the Chief of the Defence Staff."

*

They hadn't closed the curtains. Outside, the first of the morning sun turned the mountain tops to pink and Elizabeth breathed a deep and sleepy sigh and rolled against her lover. She liked to think of him as her lover. A lover was what she needed just now. She lay a hand on his stomach. Not just any lover, of course, she noticed that she had become rather particular. What she needed was this lover. She moved her hand and felt him awaken.

He smiled and she kissed his smile, letting her lips linger over his cheek and her breast push against him. One brown eye opened and closed again. Elizabeth allowed her hand to play with him, felt him breathe deeply and pull her closer. She lifted her thigh and nestled against him.

It had been so little time and yet they knew each other so well. His fingers began to brush against her - as gentle as when he touched his flowers. She closed her eyes at the thought and he took this to be a sign and moved her slowly, oh so slowly, onto him.

She clung to him tightly, feeling that sweet, almost painful sensation. She had to keep him. She had to. It was the thought of losing him as much as what he was doing to her that made the tears come.

As it had been before, when the first convulsive pleasure was over, she was able to shake away the tears, laugh and crawl all over him. She made him pick her up again, his hands under her thighs, her arms around his neck and walk around the room. They watched themselves in the mirror; he hunched over, his muscles standing out against the shining skin, she tiny and doll-like clinging onto him.

They went on until exhaustion overtook them and he rolled her - soggy and dishevelled across the bed –and still she came back at him, kneeling between his splayed thighs, working with her hands and her mouth until his toes curled and tiny primitive grunts gurgled from his throat.

"We can't stop now, you know."

"We can't?" Slowly and deliberately she spilled a tiny puddle of orange juice onto his belly and licked it off. "No, we can't. What are we going to do when I have to go back to England?"

"We will write love letters."

"Love letters. You think I'm going to be content with love letters after this."

"You haven't read my love letters. Very sexy. Compared to

me, your D.H. Lawrence is for children. You wait."

"Mmm, I don't know. I think I might appreciate something a little more solid." She allowed her hand to wander again and he caught it.

"Can't you come to England? Build some motorways for us..."

"Too easy. In England, the ground stays too flat."

She hauled herself up on one elbow and looked at him, suddenly serious: "But you could. Just for a holiday."

"But I've had my holiday."

"Have another one. Take some money out of your numbered Swiss bank account - that's if you can remember the number."

"And what will you do for me if I do?"

"This."

"Oh yes"?"

"And this."

"Hmmm?"

"And... this."

"Aaah... "

FOUR

Bernie felt slightly awkward about continuing to meet Porky Johnson at the Army and Navy Club. He hadn't liked to explain why on the telephone in case anyone might be listening. All he'd said was: "If you're in a rush we could meet in St James's Park or somewhere..."

But the Major was not going to pass up the opportunity of lunch - and particularly not the club's suet pudding.

"If you're worried about security, old man," he said as they settled at their corner table - and then waited until the steward had departed, "don't do anything different. Stick to your routine. Nobody pays any attention if you stick to your routine. Cheers."

Bernie wetted his lips and put the glass down.

The Major drank deeply. "Hell of a week, I can tell you. You'll never believe it but the Chief of the Defence Staff, no less, has refused this disarmament nonsense. Went to your chum Tattersall and told him straight. Said he wouldn't do it. Said he'd resign his commission first. What d'you think of that, eh? Bloody good show. They can have my commission too if they want it. What can they do, I ask you - bugger all. Can't very well get on with their disarmament if everyone they ask to do it promptly resigns, can they? Have another? Jolly good: MacPherson, two more of the same if you'd be so kind .... "

Bernie Price knew quite well that officers could not simply resign just because they disapproved of their orders.

It wasn't nearly as simple as that. But he asked, "Porky, are you telling me that Field Marshall Hugh-Williams has been to the Prime Minister and refused to implement disarmament?"

"That's what I said, that's the gist of things."

"I'm not asking for the gist of things, I'm asking you is that what happened. "

"Well, that's what I've heard. He wouldn't do it, that's the whisper. "

The drinks came, and Price left his standing beside the first: "Who told you?"

"Common knowledge, old man. Everyone's talking about it." That made it either untrue or a deliberate leak. Price began to deal with his drinks.

He was still sober when he got back to the office and tapped into the library for Field Marshall Hugh-Williams. Whatever you wanted to know, from the trade figures to the name of a film star's cat, it was in there somewhere.

Almost immediately the entry flashed onto the VDU screen: "Hugh-Williams, Sir James: Soldier". Price called up the cuttings onto the screen, reading them carefully one after another. They began in the l960' s with a small note in the old Times that Lieutenant James Hugh-Williams, son of Lt Col and Mrs Cecil Hugh-Williams had married Laura Fosby at the Guards Chapel. There were small mentions of his appointments: British Army on the Rhine, Northern Ireland, the Falklands Campaign in l982. There were details of his growing string of medals: OBE, CBE, CB and finally, the knighthood.

And mixed up with them were small stories of his doings throughout all this time. Price read through most of it before he found what he was looking for. There was a cutting from the Express's William Hickey diary of about a year back reporting some minor squabble over the venue for a charity ball in aid of the NSPCC. It turned out Lady Hugh-Williams was on the committee.

Next, Price went over to the bookcase at the back of the room and took down Who's Who. The big red book was renewed every year, but it still looked shabby from over-use. For the Field Marshall it gave only the address of the Ministry of Defence. That was reasonable; people who had to worry about bombs under their cars tended not to advertise their home addresses. Price took down a ten-year-old copy. The Field Marshall hadn't been so important then and his address was on the bottom of the entry.

Price went back to his desk and called directory enquiries. He gave the Field Marshall's name and address. He was told the number was ex-directory. So the old boy still lived there...

Then he phoned him at the Ministry. He put a finger on the telephone rest ready to cut himself off and told the great man's secretary: "It's Bernard Price here. Look, I don't want trouble the old man if he's busy, but I do want to catch him sometime today. "

The name Bernard Price clearly meant nothing to the girl. She was only too grateful not to have to interrupt her boss.

She said: "Well. Sir James is engaged in meetings for most of the afternoon."

"Never mind, I'll catch him at home. What time should I try do you think?"

By using the secretary's guess, his own estimate of the average speed of an official Daimler and adding half an hour for error, it was 7.30 when Price knocked on the Field Marshall's front door - quarter of an hour before he was due home.

Although Lady Hugh-Williams had never in her life seen the little man in the green tweed suit politely raising his hat, she didn't say so. Bernie Price shook her by the hand and talked solidly and with all the charm he could muster. He always felt awkward explaining who he was: People tended to edge away at the very mention of newspapers. Price's usual tactic was to swamp them with so much information that they stopped thinking logically: "We met during all that fuss over the NSPCC ball. Actually, it's your husband I've come to see - although I'm afraid I'm a bit early. Oh, that's very kind –a glass of sherry perhaps..."

And he was in. By the time the Field Marshall arrived and slotted his umbrella carefully into the hall stand, Bernie Price was sitting smiling in the drawing room with a glass of fino and listening to a whispered conversation in which Sir James seemed to be saying he had certainly not arranged to meet anyone at home while Lady Hugh-Williams insisted he was getting absent-minded in his old age.

In the end the old Soldier came into the drawing room without shaking hands and said: "I think, Mr Price, you had better tell me what this is all about."

And Price, getting up for an instant so as to appear polite and then sitting down so he would be more difficult to throw out, said: "What it is about, Sir, is that I gather the Government is so anxious to scrap nuclear weapons that they plan to do it so quickly there is considerable risk of an accident. The message I'm trying to get over is that by being too enthusiastic, Mr Tattersall is in fact increasing the risk of the very tragedy he wants to avoid."

The two men looked at each other for rather longer than was quite polite while the Chief of the Defence Staff evidently considered throwing the reporter out of the house, telling him to contact the Ministry press office - and finally decided that even though Price had entirely the wrong end of the stick, it would do no harm to put him right.

The Field Marshall began to talk.

It was late when Bernie Price got back to his flat overlooking the river at Kew. He parked in his numbered space, collected his portable computer from the boot and went up to the compact, one bedroom, one reception room apartment that was his home. It was modest by most standards but the view made it expensive.

He hung his hat on the curly stand behind the door along with its two brothers, went into the kitchen and prepared himself a cup of instant coffee and a bowl of cornflakes.

These he took into his bedroom and sat down at his desk. Never having been married, he saw nothing odd about keeping his desk in his bedroom. Then, with his little meal at his side, he began to read through his notes.

Presently he placed the computer in front of him, plugged in the mains lead to save the batteries, thought for a moment or two and then - using no more than two fingers of each hand, began to type very fast indeed.

*

At eleven O'clock the following evening the first editions of the next morning's papers were delivered to No 10 Downing Street. The duty officer took them up to the P.M.'s room and placed them quietly on the corner of the desk. Mike Tattersall, engrossed in paperwork, grunted and idly glanced at the top of the pile. The one word headline leapt up at him "MUTINY".

Above it was the line: "Service chiefs block disarmament" and underneath: "Exclusive by Bernard Price, Defence Correspondent."

The Government faces what amounts to open mutiny from the heads of the three armed services over the planned unilateral nuclear disarmament.

Chief of the Defence Staff Field Marshall Sir James Hugh-Williams has told Mr Tattersall that he would rather resign than carry out the plan and last night there was every indication that other service chiefs would do the same.

Faced with this situation the Peace Movement would have no hope of carrying out their promise to dismantle Britain's nuclear arsenal.

However, in what must surely be the most extraordinary demonstration of political power by the military, the services have offered to do a deal with the politicians.

At his home in Goring-on-Thames yesterday, Sir James explained: "If the Government will hold a referendum and the people of this country endorse, disarmament, then I will implement their decision. But until I am certain that is the wish of the country as a whole, I will continue to protect our national security with the best means at my disposal. From conversations I have had with other senior officers my impression is that it is likely they would do the same."

At the bottom of the column was the legend: "Turn to page 2 column 6." Mike Tattersall didn't bother. He knew quite well what he would find there. He pressed the button on the intercom and said: "Get me the Attorney General at home."

FIVE

Elizabeth Crichton had commandeered a conference room. It was the only way to get this sort of job done - and there was no doubt that since her holiday, she had returned to the Ministry with all her old enthusiasm. Her boss certainly seemed to have noticed it, as he had noticed - but studiously avoided - commenting on her new ash-blonde hair. He had come puffing up to her desk brandishing the third and final draft of the latest interim report on the progress of nuclear disarmament. There were 32 pages of text, maps and statistics which all had to be duplicated, checked and stapled into red folders.

It was a menial task for a higher executive officer but Elizabeth was the most junior with the security clearance to do it. A month ago she would have resented being used as little more than a junior clerical officer. Now everything was different. She dealt the sheets of paper into piles like playing cards, walking round and round the long table, thinking of Lorenz. Everything revolved around Lorenz now.

By the time the cabinet members read their copies of the report ready for tomorrow's meeting. Elizabeth would have Lorenz in her bed. She would have liked to meet him at the airport but there was a certain amount to be said for doing it his way. It meant that when they first set eyes on each other it would be in her flat with low lights, soft music and poulet basquaise on the slow cooker. All she had to do was pick up the wine on the way home. The only thing she wasn't certain about was whether she would be able to keep her hands off him long enough to drink it.

She peered absent-mindedly at a page of the report. It seemed to be concerned with missiles being kept in submarines because there was not enough storage space on shore. On another day Elizabeth might have been interested. Today she flew through her work, presenting it to Mr Perry with a beaming smile and the suggestion that since she had been so quick, she might go home early. She was out of the building and running for the bus by the time Big Ben struck 5.l5. She picked up the wine from the off licence at the corner of her road and had her key in her hand when she noticed the man getting out of the estate car.

He was foreign and ridiculously full of apologies. He came stumbling out, shutting the tail of his raincoat in the door: "Miss Crichton is it? I'm so sorry, do forgive me but I appear to have made a big mistake. You see, Lorenz said he was coming to see you..."

"Lorenz..." Suddenly she was on edge. Something had happened to Lorenz.

"No. no. nothing at all. You see it's just that he wrote and said he was coming to London and a group of us thought what a good idea to give him a surprise welcome party. Well, you know what young men are: My son Josef and some of Lorenz's old friends from Zurich, they went to collect him at the airport and it wasn't until they got him home that we realised he had special plans for this evening."

The man gestured down to Elizabeth's bag with the neck of the wine bottle poking out: "Please come and join the party. Lorenz has been most kind, he does not want to disappoint his young friends who are so pleased to see him but also he wishes very much to see you. "

Elizabeth smiled then. It was typical of Lorenz. She could imagine him being whisked away on a tide of back slapping, far too polite to protest. She said: "Yes, of course. "

He led her gently to the car and settled her in the passenger seat with her bag at her feet and then bustled round, climbing in beside her and drove off with a lurch.

He continued to chatter and made a great show, with many more apologies, of introducing himself: "Franz Zimmermann. from Zurich originally but now I live in Hammersmith. My wife is English, you see. It's quite convenient for the City, especially if you know a few short cuts."

As if on cue, he turned into one. The road was deserted between two high corrugated iron walls. Suddenly Elizabeth saw why it was deserted. It was a dead end. She was about to say so when there was a thump behind her seat. Something was moving in the estate part of the car where the seats were folded down. It occurred to her that Herr Zimmermann had a dog. But as she turned, it was a man who clutched at her head from behind. She screamed and Zimmermann said something urgent in German. She clawed at the man's hands with her nails and gulped for breath. She wanted air. The car smelled bad and then there was some sort of dank cloth across her face. She could see it so close it was out of focus - a kitchen dishcloth. It smelled awful. Sweet and sickly. The man was pressing it over her mouth and nose. But she wanted air. Oh God, it stank. She gasped, dragging the revolting smell deep down into her lungs. She felt sick and dizzy. She could see only blackness with flashes of light - and then nothing.

She felt sick.

Her face was cold and clammy. She went to wipe her forehead but found that her arm wouldn't move. She couldn't understand why. It was a long time before she thought to open her eyes.

There were people around her and German voices. Where had she heard German voices? Lorenz spoke German. Lorenz ... There was a man sitting opposite her. He seemed vaguely familiar. Suddenly Elizabeth woke up completely.

She and Lorenz were sitting opposite each other about two metres apart, each in a wooden armchair and with their wrists and ankles strapped down. She was still wearing her coat, but Lorenz was naked. In his lap his penis lay limp and soft. Biting into the smooth skin was a small silver crocodile clip with a red wire attached. On his scrotum was a second clip. This one with a black wire.

She screamed and then went on screaming and someone slapped her face and she fainted.

"Come my dear, we want to get this over with. We have no wish to cause your friend any unnecessary suffering."

The voice was gentle and full of concern. She felt confused and frightened. Herr Zimmermann was wiping her forehead with a cool damp cloth. She stared at him.

"Who are you? What are you doing?"

"Yes, questions; who and why and what. You must have many questions." He sighed, very at ease - not at all the bumbling man in the estate car.

"I regret there are many I cannot answer. I cannot tell you who I am. I cannot tell you why it is necessary for us all to be here. But I can tell you what we are going to do."

Lorenz spoke for the first time then. His voice was thick as if his tongue filled his mouth. Very slowly and with obvious effort he said: "If you lay a finger on her, I will kill you."

Zimmermann was amused. He swung round and looked closely into Lorenz's face: "My dear young man. If you stay very long in this country there is an expression you will learn. It says 'You and whose army?' I am sure I do not need to explain it.

"And now, we must get on. Plug it in." Elizabeth noticed for the first time that there was a man behind her. He must have been the one in the back of the car. He had a crew cut and wore a T-shirt. His muscles bulged like a bodybuilder's. He pushed a three-pin plug into a socket by the skirting board and as he did so, Zimmermann sat down at a table on Elizabeth's right. He was midway between her and Lorenz as if he was going to referee some kind of contest. On the table in front of him was a grey metal box with a dial, a knob and a button set in a neat row down the middle. One wire led to the wall socket, the others to the crocodile clips.

She knew what it was, and she could guess what it would do. She looked again at Lorenz. He forced a grim smile and said: "It doesn't matter. Whatever it is they want, let the bastards..."

The man in the T-shirt hit him. The blow came from the side and caught him on the temple with all the power of those obscene muscles. Lorenz's head lolled onto his chest.

Zimmermann was angry now. He spoke rapidly in German. The man in the T-shirt looked sheepish and seemed to shrink to half his size. Zimmermann turned to Elizabeth and smiled apologetically as if his dog had growled at a visitor.

"I am afraid this will delay us for a few minutes. But at least it will give me a chance to explain this apparatus to you." He patted the box in front of him. "As you are no doubt aware the normal domestic electrical supply in this country is distributed at 240 volts. If that current is passed into the human body, it causes an unpleasant muscle convulsion which we know as an electric shock. The shock from the battery of a car at l2 volts is less painful and at the other end of the scale, the shock from an overhead power cable at 22,000 volts can kill.

"What I have here is a transformer. By turning the knob I

can select whatever voltage I choose and by pressing the button I can deliver that current into the body of Herr Erhardt here."

Elizabeth shut her eyes and hung her head. But Zimmermann went on in the same conversational tone: "Of course, this is not a new development and it can be used in various ways. The electrodes for instance can be connected to almost any area of the body you choose to name - the nipples, lips, tongue - any sensitive area. In fact I understand that in some countries of South America electrodes have even been connected to the eyeballs.

"However, in view of the particular relationship between yourself and Herr Erhardt, I feel that in this case I have made the appropriate choice. For you see, I wish you to help me and to persuade you to do that I need to demonstrate how very unpleasant this technique can be... Oh come on, wake him up, can't you."

Elizabeth opened her eyes to see the man in the T-shirt bending over Lorenz, slapping his face lightly and peeling back his eyelids. Gradually, with a low groan, he came to.

Zimmermann became businesslike: "Come along. I want him fully conscious. We haven't all night."

Elizabeth began to panic. She strained at the straps around her wrists. She began to cry. She knew she was becoming hysterical and felt that was good. It would demonstrate that she would do anything for Lorenz.

She could hear herself babbling: "I'll do it. Tell me what to do. Oh God, don't hurt him. I'll do whatever you say..."

Zimmermann just nodded without looking at her: "Of course you will my dear, of course you will." And then, as Lorenz opened his eyes fully and looked at her with a trickle of blood running down his cheek, Zimmermann added, "But I think you would find it helpful if you knew precisely what will happen if you do not do exactly as you are told."

He pressed the button.

To begin with there was no sound. Lorenz's body tensed like a spring, his hands and feet stuck out grotesquely from the straps, the fingers curled and the stump of bone on his left hand showing sharp and white against the skin. Every muscle and sinew strained as his back arched like a bow and his head tilted back at the ceiling so that Elizabeth caught only a glimpse of staring pain-filled eyes and the deep black hole of a mouth.

Then came the scream. High pitched and unwavering. It was not like any scream she had ever heard. This had a horrifying animal quality - primitive, as if it stretched back thousands of years encompassing all the fear and pain of mankind. Then it subsided in gasping sobs and the body slumped back into the chair.

First Elizabeth was sick and then she fainted.

They had moved her. She was lying on a plump old sofa in an over-decorated room with heavy lampshades and a small table whose elaborate cloth reached right to the floor. Her hands and feet were no longer bound and

Zimmermann was pouring tea.

"Ah, so you are awake," he said cheerfully. "I imagine a cup of tea is just what you need. He made no attempt to hand it to her but put it on the table at her elbow.

"I'm sorry that you felt unwell. You coat, by the way has been sponged down and will be fit for you to wear again when you leave. "

She thought of hurling the cup of hot tea in his face and running - but the man in the T-shirt was standing in front of the door with his arms folded. She relaxed and then, after a moment, reached for the tea cup. It had absurd roses all round the rim but Zimmermann was right; tea was what she needed.

"What ... " she began - and then didn't know how to go on.

"What have I done with your friend Lorenz? He is safely locked away. Don't be alarmed. He has come to no permanent harm. When all this is over you can have him back and I'm sure you will find that the particular piece of anatomy on which we have concentrated so much this evening... "

She threw the cup at him.

Zimmermann barked an order even as he flung up his arm to protect himself - but still the scalding liquid hit him full in the face.

Elizabeth launched herself after the cup, her teeth and nails bared. But the man in the T-shirt plucked her out of mid-air and stood holding her pinioned by the arms.

Zimmermann was cursing in German and mopping at himself with a handkerchief. One side of his face was red and blotchy. He came up in front of her and slapped her twice across the face, hard.

The tears started in her eyes and she knew she was beaten. Miserably she allowed herself to be flung back on the sofa and sat there sobbing while Zimmermann went on: "Very well, if you have no wish to be civilised about this, there is another way. Come, sit here...

Roughly, he cleared away the tea things and made a place for her.

"Now, you asked me why you are here - what is the purpose of all this. Now I will tell you. Miss Crichton, you are a more important young lady that you realise. You work in the office of the Permanent Secretary to the Minister of Defence. There you see many important papers. I too wish to see those papers."

She stared at him. It had simply never occurred to her. She had had so many warnings. There had been lectures and circulars...

"You're a spy," she said stupidly. Zimmermann stopped suddenly and looked at her in surprise: "Why yes, Miss Crichton, and so are you - or at least you will be very soon."

She almost said: "I won't do it," but instantly knew she would. Instead she sat there and listened while he told her what she would do.

She would search out any papers to do with nuclear weapons - anything at all. She would duplicate them and smuggle the copies out of the building. Did she understand?

She nodded and he looked straight into her eyes until she had to look away. Then he got up and fetched a small suitcase from the corner of the room. Inside it was a complicated-looking electric typewriter. He unravelled the lead and plugged it in. "You can type?"

"Yes."

"Excellent. There will be a lot of typing to do. When you bring the documents home, you will type them onto this machine. It has no paper but the words come up here on the screen - you see? That is so you will know if you make a mistake.

"You will type all the documents one after another, everything. Then, when you have finished you will set up this little aerial and press this button here. It will stay down for a moment or two and then pop up again - and in that time "zip"" everything you have typed will be transmitted to another machine which will be... well you do not need to know where.

"Both of us will be safe from detection. You, because your transmission will be so quick that anyone listening will assume it is no more than atmospheric static - and I will be safe because you will not know where I am.

"This arrangement has been worked out most carefully. The worst you could do would be to simply not transmit the documents at all. And if that happened, you know what would happen to Herr Erhardt, don't you?"

She nodded once more. Then, sitting listlessly and helplessly at the little, old fashioned table, she allowed him to teach her to use the machine. When he was satisfied he packed it up in its case and the other man brought her coat, smelling strongly of disinfectant and with a large damp patch down the front. She stood up and took the machine and faced Zimmermann. She was surprised to find they were virtually the same height. "All right," she said. "I'll do it. But I want to know who you are. Where this information is going." He smiled and made a gesture of the shoulders. "You're Russian aren't you. You're going to send this to Moscow. "

"I am a citizen of the Soviet Union, yes. There is no harm in your knowing what anyone would guess."

"And one more thing. I want to see Lorenz - alone."

Zimmermann smiled his disarming smile again and said: "I am afraid that will not be possible."

But there was a recklessness about her now. She had gone so low there was no other way but up. She stared him dumbly straight in the eye and slowly relaxed the fingers of her right hand.

The little suitcase fell to the floor with an ominous rattle.

The effect was most satisfying. At first, she thought he was going to hit her again. His face became mottled but then, with an effort, he controlled himself. Slowly he picked up the case and put it on the table.

"Wait here."

He left her with the silent man in the T-shirt and she sat

down on the sofa again. She considered trying to escape but that was pointless because they were going to let her go anyway. What she had to do was tell Lorenz that she was going to beat these people. She had no idea how but something must be possible. She stared at the man in the T-shirt with what she hoped was defiance. But he just stared back as if she didn't exist.

Zimmermann came back and made her walk in front of him down to the cellar. The man in the T-shirt let her in and closed the door behind her.

Lorenz lay on his side on an old-fashioned bed with a polished walnut headboard. He had his hands thrust between his legs.

"Oh God. Elizabeth. what's happening?"

She went and sat with him on the bed. She took his head in her lap and stroked his brow. He looked up at her - his eyes searching her face. She felt him shaking.

"What do they want?" he asked her. "Why are they doing this"?"

"They want me to spy for them. They're Russians."

"You mustn't."

"Oh yes. my love... I must. I won't let them hurt you again. I promise."

She eased herself down on the bed and gradually he unfolded his leg's until they were lying in each other's arms, tasting the tears on each other's cheeks just as they had before, when they had been happy.

*

The man who called himself Zimmermann walked back into the room a little after ten.

Without taking off his coat he went straight to the cocktail cabinet and poured himself a whisky. Standing there, he drank it down in one.

Only then did he turn and gesture with the empty glass to Lorenz. The younger man looked up from the sofa and smiled: "Are we celebrating then?"

"I do believe we are. We took her blindfold off and kicked her out of the car somewhere in Mayfair. She went off like a lamb. Your performance, by the way... quite masterful. You deserve an Oscar. "

"Or the Order of Lenin."

"That too. "

They drank. Lorenz toyed with his glass for a moment and then said: "All the same I wasn't very happy with that curtain call. We should have been ready for that. For a moment I thought she was going to dress my wounds."

Zimmermann laughed a harsh braying laugh. But he added: "She is not quite what we've been led to expect. There is more spirit there than I would have liked. I think we may have a little trouble with her - nothing we can't handle, but ... " he made a gesture with his hand, "a little trouble..."

SIX

The King was shaving when he heard the news on the radio. It was depressingly brief: *RAF Regiment guards last night fired several shots when a large number of demonstrators broke into the Royal Air Force station at Henington in Suffolk. It is understood that no-one was hurt.*

Some military equipment was damaged but the demonstrators were prevented from reaching the bunkers where nuclear weapons are stored. Several arrests have been made.

So finally, it had happened. The two sides which believed so passionately in peace and worked so hard for it in their own very different ways, were now fighting each other.

The news came in slowly, in bits and pieces so that he kept the radio on over breakfast which he knew would annoy the Queen who liked to talk.

It was astonishing the lengths these people had gone to. The nuclear bases, ever since the days of Greenham Common, were designed like fortresses with stainless steel barbed wire, floodlights and watchtowers. But apparently these people had dug a tunnel.

A spokeswoman for the protesters gave an interview. The tunnel, she said, had been started the previous year and abandoned when the Peace Movement won the election. But now, after Field Marshall Hugh-Williams' comments in the press, it had been opened up again to show that "The People" wanted action now.

There was a telephone interview with a back-bench MP

who said he could quite understand why it had happened. He now envisaged more people taking the law into their own hands.

The King could see it already. There would come a time when warning shots would not be enough. Before long someone was going to get killed - and when that happened you had a climate in which some countries dissolved into civil war and others experienced military takeovers.

It happened, of course, because the dispute was always between the men at the heads of the two factions. There could never be a mediator because there was no-one above them and the international community never wanted to get involved until it was too late.

But Great Britain was not like other countries. Great Britain was a monarchy. For as long as anyone could remember that had meant little more than a rather quaint excuse for national pride. But that was only because for hundreds of years Britain had been a well-ordered country where things like this never happened. There had been no need for the monarch in the constitutional sense.

Well, now there was.

That was why the constitution provided the Royal Prerogative: The King still had the power to dissolve Parliament at any time simply by issuing a proclamation. It had happened with the Australian Parliament only 20 years before and there had been times when Prime Ministers had been refused a dissolution and forced to soldier on.

But to order a new election so soon after the country had been to the polls smacked horribly of dictatorship by proxy - of allowing the people the choice only if they made the right choice.

No, he couldn't do that.

The one thing he needed to do - simply to call for a referendum, was the one thing that was not within his power - yet all the same he did have a right no-one else in the country possessed: He had the right to make the Prime Minister and the Chief of the Defence Staff listen to him. He might not sway them, he might not bring them together - but as he sat there over his largely uneaten breakfast, he was convinced that at this moment in Britain's history, the monarch had a role to play. He had a role to play. He looked up as people do when they've reached a difficult decision, and he saw the Queen. She had been sitting watching him and now her face was gently serious.

She said: "It's Tuesday."

"Yes," said the King. "Tuesday. Prime Minister's audience."

Michael Tattersall had taken to arriving just a minute or two late. The inference had not been lost on the King. This time he was early - and he was angry.

The King asked him when he would be meeting the Chief of the Defence Staff again. He added: "Some middle way must be found, "

Tattersall's head jerked up: "It's got nothing to do with

any middle way. There is absolutely no reason why the Government should compromise."

"You're going to allow what happened last night to happen again?"

"It's not a question of the Government allowing it - the military are provoking it. What do you expect people to do. If democracy doesn't work? They have to try something else."

Possibly for the first time the King had to agree with him. He said: "Exactly. On both sides there are people who don't know what else they can do. That's why we must find a way out. Now a referendum... "

"A referendum - of course - the old chestnut. Forgive me, sir, but I was rather expecting we'd get to that. Did you know the campaign's already started? Oh yes, the campaign to prove to the public that the Russians are just waiting for their chance to attack us. There's even an intelligence report giving chapter and verse."

He paused for effect and smiled at the King's obvious surprise: "Oh yes, it's all par for the course. A lot of wishful thinking by the would-be James Bonds of the Intelligence Service - but not a shred of evidence. And quite frankly if I'm provoking that sort of reaction then I know I'm on the right track."

The King did not argue with him after that. In fact he ushered him out with an impression of haste that Tattersall seemed to take as an admission of defeat.

But even so it was after lunch before the correct written

authorities had been delivered to the correct offices and a special courier with an armed military escort arrived at Buckingham Palace with a briefcase handcuffed to his wrist.

The papers it contained did not give any conclusive evidence but at the same time they could hardly be ignored:

The account began in l981 when Poland was in turmoil as the trade union Solidarity won concession after concession from the Government. Moscow watched with growing concern from one side and the West with eager anticipation from the other - and a young Red Army Captain called Yuri Markov reached a momentous decision. He had been uneasy about the invasion of Afghanistan when he had assisted in drawing up plans for logistical support. Now he was called on to do the same to prepare the Red Army for an operation to bring the Poles to heel.

But young Markov could not bring himself to believe in it. Here was a situation where a people were fighting for the right to determine their own future. It was a cause as noble as the one his grandfather had fought for during the Revolution. Yet now young Yuri was being asked to play his part in crushing that same spirit.

He thought first of sabotage, of sending his supplies to the wrong destinations. But that, if it had any effect at all, could lead to the deaths of thousands of his comrades. What he had to do was stop the invasion altogether - so Yuri Markov wrote a letter. He wrote it in Russian since he knew no Polish, but he wrote to Pope John Paul II warning him of what was about to happen and urging him to make "A gesture of resolve." That, he explained, would be enough.

He signed it with his name rank and number, added for good measure, his address and even stamped it with the stamp of the Red Army Directorate of Supply. Someone would have to take notice.

Then he carried it around with him, waiting for a chance to deliver it. The risk he took was enormous. But eventually he passed it to the first Western diplomat he could find - the British Military Attaché.

The Embassy sent a copy to London in the diplomatic bag and the original went to Rome. The following day a letter from the Pope was dispatched by special emissary to the Kremlin. His Holiness had resolved that, in the event of a Soviet invasion of Poland, he would lay down the crown of St Peter and fight to defend his homeland.

When, after a month, the units of the Red Army on manoeuvres within 100 miles of the Polish border, were still no closer to Warsaw and Yuri Markov was told to microfilm the supply schedules and shred the originals, he wondered if it really had been because of his letter or whether this was the way things would have turned out anyway.

In the years that followed, he rose steadily, as a hard-working young man will rise through the ranks of the Soviet military machine. He married an attractive statistician and began to move in increasingly distinguished circles of Moscow Society. Eventually he emerged at the top of the pile as Commander of the Red Army Directorate of Supply.

His wife was pleased. So were those friends who were not in direct competition with him - but the most pleased of all were the men who ran the British Secret Intelligence Service. To begin with it had been necessary to show Markov the copy of his letter as he vacillated, tried to refuse instructions and - as one report to London suggested - attempted suicide. But as time went on he came to accept his role as a spy. The psychiatrist's report had said this would happen, that he would come to terms with his treachery by convincing himself that it was all for the good of mankind.

By the time he reached the pinnacle of his career, Yuri Markov had become that most useful of agents - a spy motivated by conviction.

What he heard at the meeting of the central committee of the Army High Command, horrified him. He was presented with a list of objectives - objectives deep within Western Europe. Dates on a timetable that would take Soviet Forces to the farthest extremities of Ireland and Spain. Anything more than token resistance was to be met first by a warning and then the detonation of a small nuclear device over a provincial city.

The High Command expected to have to make an example early in the campaign and a list of possible targets was included with the briefing. The generals discussed the plan with great enthusiasm. Markov felt sickened.

Twenty-four hours after that meeting the preliminary details of the Soviet strategy were on the desk of the head of Britain's Secret Intelligence Service.

*

No-one ever remembered Detective Inspector Donald Carling. He was the shadow who walked one pace to the side of the Prime Minister at all times, who got out of the car first, before it stopped moving, whose eyes scanned crowds and who accepted as part of the job that he was the one who was supposed to get his body between the boss and an assassin's bullet.

What the Prime Minister told him now, he accepted without a murmur.

Tattersall leaned over the desk and said: "I want you to do a special job for me. I want you to do it without telling anyone else, without reporting to Scotland Yard - I want this kept completely secret."

Carling said: "Yes Sir."

"I want you to find out who's involved in this campaign by the military. This is only the beginning, believe me. They want us out and sooner or later they're going to find a way to get us out. I want to know what they're up to. I want to know who's masterminding it, who I can trust and who I can't. I want to know what I'm up against, Inspector."

Carling waited for him to finish. Then he said: "You'd do

better to give it to MI5, Sir. They're used to that sort of thing, they've got all the equipment and they've got the manpower too. This would be quite an operation - round the clock surveillance on all the senior officers for a start."

But Tattersall wouldn't have it. The initials of MI5 stood for "Military Intelligence" - it would be like asking the Army to investigate itself.

"Do the best you can on your own, just for the moment. Depending on what you turn up, we'll think about extending the thing. But for the moment the fewer who know about it the better. "

He nodded to indicate that Carling was dismissed. Then he added: "I will of course see you're paid something extra for this. "

The detective was at the door and he stopped and turned. He didn't say a word but just looked at the Prime Minister. If the look had lasted a moment longer it would have been insolent. Instead he went out and closed the door quietly behind him.

*

It was easy, really. Elizabeth's first attempt at spying had made her hands shake and the hair on the back of her neck stand on end. But it really was surprisingly easy.

She was running the report through the copier when Mr Perry came fussing up: "What are you doing, Miss Crichton. "That's a restricted document."

She smiled sweetly and explained that when it came to checking the figures against the department's own records, it would never do to mark the original. She would shred the copy as soon as she had finished with it.

Mr Perry sniffed, but he went away, looking for some other irregularity to uncover.

When Elizabeth had finished she did indeed take the copy to the room at the end of the corridor where a shredding machine turned much of Whitehall's output into paper spaghetti. But on the way she passed the ladies and popped in.

The report, folded into four, slipped into the waistband of her skirt and lay against the small of her back under her jacket. The other sheaf of paper, the old memos which had collected in her bottom drawer, would never be read by anyone again.

For an hour or two the report seemed to burn into her back almost as if it was as radioactive as the weapons themselves. But after a while she forgot about it entirely. It was only as she left the building and smiled goodnight to the security man that she felt once again that tingle of danger. As she stepped out of the building she was intrigued to find that she rather liked it.

She spent the evening typing. The green dot danced before her eyes, dragging out the words - the secrets she was giving to Moscow. It had never occurred to her that every day she handled documents which could be dangerous if they got into the wrong hands. What would the Russians do with them? Would they store them away in their files? Was the whole thing a vast clerical exercise - surely not.

For the Russians to go to all this trouble, these figures must be vitally important to them. Whatever it was they were planning, they had to have these exact figures.

Elizabeth stopped and poured herself a glass of wine. She came back and stood looking at the neat columns. If statistics were really so important. then supposing she gave the wrong ones - the whole document would become worthless.

That was it. She could do it with everything, with memos and reports and lists, changing words and figures, making a nonsense of the whole business - and they would never know. It was the answer...

Eagerly she put down her wine and began from where she had left off, transposing figures, adding here, subtracting there. Happy and relaxed, she typed steadily for an hour. Then she set up the aerial, pressed the button, watched it pop up again and went to bed.

She was asleep when the phone rang.

Zimmermann.

She snapped awake at once. Lorenz would be there. They would let her talk to Lorenz.

But they didn't. Zimmermann waited only long enough to make sure he had the right number, then he began: "You have been foolish. Do you think I cannot add up?"

She could hear a scuffling in the background. She tried to

explain, not knowing how she would explain. She begged, she pleaded - and then the scream came. It rattled the earpiece. It seemed to drive deep into her head. It broke off into pitiful sobs.

"God no, no ... " But Zimmermann ignored her: "Do it again. You have one hour."

The line went dead. The call had lasted just 30 seconds. With tears rolling down her face and making the keys slippery under her fingers, she typed out the report all over again and sent it.

She stayed awake for the rest of the night, crying to herself, waiting for the phone to ring. But it never did.

TRIDENT

SEVEN

The King said: "I don't want you to leave Beech Lodge."

It was something Vice Admiral Sir Charles Lomas had been expecting and he had his speech all ready: "My mind's made up, Sir. If I'm to resign my commission, it wouldn't be right for me to stay in your house... "

The King said: "I don't want you to resign your commission either."

And then he added: "Do you want one more job, Charles?"

And that's how it had started. It was obvious now that the whole business - the lunch, the discussion of the political situation - the extraordinary insight into the findings of the intelligence service - even the King's private fears for the way the country was heading - it had all been leading up to this.

The King looked out of the mullioned window to where the sun blazed down in the courtyard and went on gently: "There is an alternative you know. Suppose we were to maintain an independent nuclear deterrent - one Trident submarine kept out of the hands of the Government while all the other nuclear weapons were scrapped. A submarine kept at sea, unknown to the people; unknown even, to the Prime Minister - and yet ready to be brought back into service at a moment's notice if the country should need it. Then there would be no civil unrest and yet, if we were threatened, we would not be defenceless."

He paused and Sir Charles tried to say something. He could think of nothing appropriate. It all sounded so.... well, crazy.

The King nodded: "Yes. I know it's well beyond our normal democratic processes. But think of this: If we were threatened I doubt very much that the public would complain they had been duped - and Parliament, I'm willing to bet, would be only to too glad to be able to reveal a deterrent in the nick of time.

"And then there are the Americans. Their decision to remain neutral would no longer apply and I imagine we would find ourselves with a powerful ally. On the other hand, if - as Mr Tattersall insists - the Russians do not have any warlike intentions, what have we lost: Nothing but our faith in our own judgement."

He stopped then and let it all sink in. For a long moment Sir Charles sat and stared at him. All he could think of saying was: "It's incredible. I mean, to steal a submarine because that's what it amounts to - and hide it away, fully operational, properly supplied for heaven knows how long... Are you sure you know what's involved, Sir? It's a massive undertaking.

"And if you're worried about civil unrest now, imagine what would happen if this got out. No, the whole thing's absolutely..."

"Absolutely mad?" The King smiled. "Yes. I thought so, too - at first. But who says it can't be done? For a start, hiding a submarine is the easiest thing in the world - that's what it's designed for. Secondly, a modern nuclear submarine can cruise virtually indefinitely. It's limited only by the amount of food it can carry.

"And as for as for what might happen if any of this leaked out ...well, if it transpired that the damage to the country looked like being greater than the risk we run in doing without a deterrent, then we could always recall the submarine and that would be the end of the matter.

"But I'm not sure anyone does need to find out. Submarines have been lost at sea in the past. Surely it would be possible to stage some sort of "accident".

The Admiral considered all this and shook his head. Whichever way he looked at it, the idea still seemed crazy - and yet, he had to admit that the alternative might not bear thinking about either.

"I don't know," he said. "The idea of a submarine just conveniently sinking and with nuclear missiles aboard, too. I hardly think they'd just forget about it. I'll have to think about this."

The King got up and said: "Do that." Sir Charles followed suit and, as they shook hands he looked his monarch in the eye and said: "Why me, sir?"

"Because you're not a serving officer. You can say no. If I asked someone else it would become an order and besides, you have a son commanding a submarine."

Sir Charles nodded slowly. It all fell into place. It had all been carefully worked out.

The King went on: "You see, Charles, the whole thing

must be done without official orders. If the worst comes to the worst, it must look like the work of a few deranged men. Officially, I would have to disown you - you might as well know that now."

"Yes Sir."

"But unofficially, will you trust me?"

*

It was within an hour of dusk. A light westerly wind came off the Isle of Arran and it was still warm enough for shirts sleeves. Peter Lomas stood with his hands behind him and the tiller pressed into his back as he guided the little white yacht into the anchorage at Lamlash.

He had dropped the mainsail and now the genoa gave him just enough speed to slide between the moorings. Johnny and Clare sat side by side on the forehatch in their lifejackets, content to look at the boats as Clarinda moved silently by. Susan was below frying onions. the smell wafted out of the companionway.

He ought to be content: This was three days embarkation leave he had allowed himself -although that hardly seemed appropriate. He already knew his orders would be to keep HMS Vanguard tied up to the jetty at Faslane.

Susan passed out a gin without saying anything. He knew she found him preoccupied and that she was waiting patiently for him to unburden himself. He wanted to - God knows. But this ...

The last thing Father had said as they parted at the gate of the little house at Windsor was: "Think about it but for Christ sake don't tell anyone."

Fat chance of that. He doubted whether anyone would believe him. The whole thing was just incredible. Things like this didn't happen in England.

But then if everything Father had told him was true, what choice did he have? Standing there with the last of the sun on his back and his family around him, the first strands of a conscious decision began to lock together in his mind.

*

The detective put the cassette player on the Prime Minister's desk and said: "Something you ought to hear, sir. Recorded by directional microphone: The Flag Officer Submarines, Eastern Atlantic - Vice Admiral Sir Geoffrey Roberts. The second voice you'll hear is a retired naval officer, a Sir Charles Lomas.

He pressed the "play" button and a man's voice, cultured and authoritative, filled the room: "...

proper mess. No-one seems to know what they're supposed to be doing any more. I have officers coming to me asking whether or not they're to give this information or that set of figures to the Ministry. I mean, what am I supposed to say?"

"What do you say?"

"Tell them it's up to them, of course. A matter for their

consciences. There's a lot of that sort of thing going on after what Hugh-Williams said. Frankly it's a shambles."

The other man appeared to lower his voice: "That's what I came to see you about, Geoffrey. There's a way out of this..."

Tattersall leaned closer. He listened intently until the end of the tape. Then he sat in silence for a long time. He knew these people would fight but he had never dreamed it would come to this. He had half a mind to tell Carling to let them carry on with their plans just to see how far they would really go - how, indeed, they intended to make a submarine disappear into thin air.

But the situation was too serious for games. He looked up at the big detective and said: "Arrest them. Do it quietly and take them somewhere where I can see them privately. I'd like to meet these two."

"Sir."

"And Carling: I want you to find the others."

As the detective made to leave, he reached over to pick up the recorder. Tattersall put his hand over it. For a minute he sat in thought. Then he pressed the intercom button and said: "Please ask the Minister of Defence to come over straight away." Then he re-wound the tape and listened to it again.

He played it a third time for Vincent Earlham. The old man was plainly horrified: "Even in my wildest nightmares. I never imagined the military were capable of something like this. Of course, it's only a minority of deranged officers.

It's not representative..."

Tattersall had not really expected him to see it any other way: "Vincent," he said. "You're a fool. You think everyone is as noble and decent as yourself.

"I want those submarines taken out of the hands of the Navy at once. Put them in civilian dockyards. Send them to Vickers at Barrow. They built the bloody things, let them take them to pieces. And I want you to assemble a team to render those missiles safe right now. If Aldermaston won't do it, try France. We're going to do this thing and we're going to do it before anyone else has any smart ideas."

*

The Assistant Commissioner said: "You might like to see how important you've become."

He pushed a piece of Home Office notepaper across the desk. It was signed by the Home Secretary himself. It said: "I should be grateful if you would afford Detective Inspector Carling any facility he might request in connection with a special inquiry which he is undertaking on the direct orders of the Prime Minister. It is not necessary for you to know the nature of the inquiry."

Carling laid it back on the desk and said: "Thank you, Sir."

The Deputy Assistant Commissioner, the man who ran Scotland Yard's Special Branch very much along the lines of a private army, said: "This department has a very high reputation, Inspector. You know that, you're part of it. You also know that it's based on teamwork. If any one of us starts branching out and doing his own thing, pretty soon we're going to end up tripping over each other.

"I won't interfere and I'll give you all the back-up you need but I think you do owe me an explanation, no matter what the Home Secretary says."

Carling nodded. Then he said: "I'm sorry, sir. But I'm under specific orders."

He did not add: "And so are you". But as he looked at the boss, he could tell what was going through his mind - that a Home Secretary could break a Deputy Assistant Commissioner no matter how much support he had at the Yard. The only thing left was to appeal to Carling's loyalty - something that should have been beyond question.

Carling had no doubt that when all this was over and Tattersall was gone from Downing Street, today would be remembered. The DAC didn't need to say anything. He just looked long and coldly across the desk and said: "Very well then, Inspector. What exactly is it you want?"

And Carling, ignoring the sarcasm, took a slip of paper from his top pocket: "I'd like these officers placed on indefinite attachment to me, sir. And I'd also like Meadowlands - again indefinitely."

With studied care, the DAC made a note on his pad. Meadowlands was the pride of the Special Branch "safe houses". It came complete with its own security staff and had survived a whole series of budget cuts.

The Deputy Assistant Commissioner went on: "Was there anything else?

Carling looked him in the eye and said: "The Prime Minister did ask me to pass on to you, sir, the importance of there being no interference in this operation. I'm sure you understand, sir. "

"Oh yes, inspector. I understand."

Their eyes met and the detective felt the warning going through his mind: *I'm finished. Win or lose, no matter how this goes, I've had it.*

And then he got up and, very calmly, he said: "Thank you, sir, "

As he rode down in the lift there was a young constable who looked at him curiously. It was only later that he realised he must have been murmuring to himself: "Just do the damn job. Don't worry, don't think. Just do it."

*

The tyres of the official Daimler made expensive crunching noises up the drive. Michael Tattersall knew such houses existed - "Safe Houses" they were called on the reports from the security services - but he had never actually seen one.

He had to admit it was ideal for the purpose - not exactly a stately home, but a very fine country house set in extensive grounds so that it was shielded from view and accessible only through high, wrought iron gates where a uniformed security man checked the driver's pass and looked into the car, raising his hand in salute to Tattersall.

Carling himself was waiting at the door. He led the way through to the back of the house and a room that was completely unfurnished but for a pair of kitchen chairs where two old men sat in shirtsleeves, bound hand and foot. One seemed to be unconscious, his head lolling forward. The other stared malevolently back at Tattersall through puffy bloodshot eyes. There was a smear of blood on his collar. It looked very much as though he had been cleaned up to meet the Prime Minister.

Tattersall took one quick look round the room, taking in the two other men who stood behind the chairs, turned on his heel and walked out.

By the time Carling joined him in the hall, the Prime Minister's anger had built itself up to a high level of controlled rage. He rounded on the detective: "What the devil do you think you're doing in there?"

At first Carling seemed genuinely surprised: "Interrogation, sir."

"Interrogation!" Tattersall could feel his voice trembling: "You call that licensed sadism "Interrogation". Now listen to me. Mr Detective Carling: I gave you a brief - to find out what those poor old fools were up to. I didn't give you permission to exercise your obscene warped pleasures on them."

Carling showed no emotion - neither remorse nor apology. He just said: "You did want to know who else was involved, sir. This is the surest way of finding out."

Tattersall looked at him sharply. It was possible the man was right - and there was no doubt that the history of the Peace Movement was full of examples of his own people being beaten up by the police. He grunted to himself and went on: "Well, since you insist it's so effective, what have you discovered?"

For the first time Carling seemed embarrassed. He said: "As things worked out this time, sir, not a lot. One of them clearly knows nothing, and the other's holding out on us. It shouldn't take much longer, though."

For a moment Tattersall was tempted to nod solemnly and tell Carling to get on with it. But it was no good, you couldn't dodge responsibility like that.

He said: "No, there'll be no more of that. I'll talk to him."

*

Charles Lomas had never been tortured before. He supposed that being tied up and beaten about the head did amount to torture. It was difficult to think clearly. For a moment, when the Prime Minister walked in, he thought he was hallucinating.

But it really was Tattersall, he could be sure now. The young man came back into the room looking anxious and giving orders to the guards. The Admiral made an effort to lift his head and tried to think of something to say.

A moment later he was too astonished to speak even if he had thought of something. First his hands and feet were released and then he was given a drink of water - he had no idea how thirsty he had become. He was taken into another room where there were armchairs and pictures on the walls and there they gave him a glass of whisky. He drank it while the Prime Minister paced up and down on the hearthrug apologising.

Sir Charles felt the whisky burn his stomach and tried to come to terms with the situation. In due course, he supposed, he would have cracked - now it was over he could afford to consider the possibility. And yet here was this man Tattersall, behaving like a mother hen and saying: "This has all been a terrible misunderstanding. I don't know how to apologise. I won't have people treated like this. I won't have it. Your friend has been put to bed and a doctor called. I can't say how sorry I am."

Sir Charles stared back at him and said nothing. Tattersall went on: "Nothing can excuse your treatment - but at the same time there's no excuse for what you intended to do. I may as well tell you now that your ridiculous plan will come to nothing. I'm taking the submarines out of the hands of the Navy right away - and you're going to stay here until I'm certain you can do no more harm. I shouldn't imagine it will be longer than 24 hours - 36 at the most."

An idea began to form at the back of Sir Charles mind. The trouble was that his mind was so shaken and bruised that he had trouble working out quite what it was. He found himself clearing his throat with a grunting noise. Finally, he said: "I see. First it's a beating and now detention without trial. I suppose this is the Peace and Freedom your people are always talking about. I want to see my solicitor."

Tattersall became even more apologetic: "I assure you, you will not be charged with any offence and you will be free to go just as soon as the submarines are safely in dockyard hands. You'll be well looked after - you have my word on it. "

But Sir Charles pressed on: "Surely you'll let me make a telephone call. I am expected home, you know. If I don't turn up my housekeeper will start phoning all the hospitals."

Tattersall considered this for a moment. He clearly didn't like the idea but whether it was his conscience that bothered him or the thought of his tarnished public image, Sir Charles couldn't tell. Anyway, he got his telephone call.

He had to think quickly now. There was clearly no point in expecting old Mrs Morley to pick up cryptic clues. He'd have to get her to pass a message to someone who would. Tattersall handed him the phone and made him wait while Carling picked up the extension. He dialled his home number.

"Hello, Mrs Morley - yes, look I won't be back tonight. I've had to go away for a few days. Now, I've invited my son and daughter-in-law for the weekend. I may not be back in time. Would you ring and warn them I may be late. You might ask my son to fix the stable door while he's there - I wasn't able to close it before I left. Thank you. Goodbye then."

He put the phone down quickly before Mrs Morley had time to realise what he had said and began to ask questions. He did not keep horses. He did not even have a stable - but these people were not to know that. They knew he lived in the country, they would think it natural enough. He only hoped Peter would grasp the significance - that the horse was about to bolt.

EIGHT

The Commodore was sorry. He had tried - a great many people had tried - but there was nothing more anyone could do.

And Peter Lomas sat with the three other submarine captains and watched everything fall into place. He had no doubt at all that if anything explained his father's disappearance this was it.

As the Commodore began to read through the schedules for departure and the procedure for handing over the submarines to the dockyard authorities, Lomas looked out to where Vanguard lay at the quay, long and black and still.

Once the missiles were hoisted out of those hatches, it would be the end of the nuclear deterrent. Lomas knew that the arguments running through his mind were the ideas fed to him during a lifetime in the service. He knew there were a great many people who would now rejoice that the world had become a safer place. But he knew it hadn't. This was being forced through by a noisy minority and soon it would be too late for anyone to stop it.

By the time the Commodore shook each man's hand and said again that he was sorry, Lomas had made up his mind.

The seaman on duty on the casing saluted and gave him the sort of penetrating look that confirmed the whole base knew the four CO's had been summoned to the Commodore. The rumour factory was now geared up to supply the reason.

He went below without a word, passing the junior rates dining hall where two dozen earnest young faces stared back at him with the same question. He walked aft to the wardroom and half a dozen of his officers got up and stood waiting.

He said: "We have our sailing orders, gentlemen. Departure is at l400. The unarmed boat go first direct to Barrow. Then Vigilant to disembark her missiles at Coulport and then us.

Wilder, the executive officer said: "For Coulport. Aye-aye, sir. "

Lomas added: "Call me when Vigilant is clear." Then he went to his cabin. He had a shower and changed his shirt. Then, as an afterthought, he checked through his seagoing kit, stowed in readiness all those weeks ago. By the time he'd finished, the phone bleeped and he went up to the bridge. Vanguard was alone at the jetty now. Half a mile down the loch, Vigilant was a lengthening pencil of grey as she turned westward through the narrows at Rosneath.

The officer of the watch waited for orders and the deck parties on the casing looked up to the bridge. Then, without fuss, Lomas edged the submarine away from the quay.

It was only when he had settled her on course for the narrows that he looked back up the loch. It was a habit with him. Every time he went to sea he always turned and raised his binoculars and looked back up the loch because out here, in the middle, he could see the old grey house and sometimes, if she knew the time of his departure, Susan might be waving in the garden. Not today, though...

Better this way, he told himself as he turned to face the sea.

If Lomas had known how the Navy would react to Vanguard's disappearance he would still have dived while heading north as if he was going out into the Atlantic through the North Channel. He would still have doubled back and gone deep - and slowed to four knots, creeping along the bottom at walking pace with the sonar room listening for the slightest sound of pursuit.

The Captain of a ballistic missile submarine is not interested in whether he is found by a friend or an enemy. To be found is to have failed - it's as simple as that. So to begin with Lomas did not wonder whether his father had made progress with the Admiralty or whether Vanguard would have the back-up she would need. Instead, he concentrated on losing himself in the Irish Sea.

It was only later, when he was well south and apparently clear that he went forward to address as many of the crew as Wilder could pack into the junior rates' recreation space. He told them straight away that they would be in for a long patrol - probably breaking a few records along the way. He reminded them of what the Chief of the Defence Staff had said about a referendum and he told them as best he could that they were going to stay at sea until the Government called one.

He paused then and nobody moved. He added: "This is,

of course a volunteer-only operation. If any of you feel you don't want to come along then I'll put you ashore - and I promise it won't count against you. Think it over and if you want to transfer to other duties come and see me by 1200 tomorrow. Come and see me anyway if you just want to talk about it. That is all."

Lomas had not expected that anyone would want to jump ship. When noon came the following day he stepped into the navigation centre, closed the door behind him and took out the chart of the North Atlantic, Eastern Section.

*

Outside the gates of Coulport, Dorothy Dean watched the last of the submarines appear at the entrance to Loch Long five miles away. Mrs Dean, a grandmother and co-founder of the Peace Camp at Coulport, had been watching submarines come and go ever since the women had moved up from Greenham Common and Molesworth when the Americans left.

Now it was all happening again. The women cheered and hugged each other. Dorothy felt good, with a sort of warm glow inside. It was very nearly over. She would be able to go home - the notion seemed so unusual she couldn't quite imagine what it would be like to go home permanently, not just for weekends and holidays. She watched the black shape move further out from the land. This would be the other one that still had its missiles. She saw the silhouette shorten as it made the turn up towards her.

Somebody pushed a pottery mug full of sparkling wine into her hand. There was a great deal of noise all about her and someone had started to sing "Can't kill the Spirit" but Dorothy barely heard the words. There was something terribly wrong. The last submarine wasn't coming up the loch towards her. It was getting smaller. It was going away.

*

The research officer at the London headquarters of the Peace Movement listened politely to Mrs Dean. He was always polite when people at peace camps claimed they had uncovered some scandal or other. In fact the research officer spent a good deal of his time chasing unsubstantiated rumours.

But he was still polite. He made a full note of everything Mrs Dean told him about a submarine which seemed to have set off to sea with all its missiles - and then he left it on his head of department's desk.

The Head of the Research Department returned in the late afternoon. He was only too aware of the significance of HMS Vanguard: This was one of the two submarines which still had its missiles aboard because the Navy insisted there was no room to store them at the armaments depot. The Head of the Research Department immediately called the National Officer.

But the National Officer had left early and was at that

moment on his way home. When he finally listened to the message on his answering machine, he decided he would rather read the report himself before taking any action. After all, it did sound rather odd: Either the Navy had decided to co-operate or it hadn't - and if it hadn't, then the submarines would never have left the base in the first place. And so it was almost 24 hours after HMS Vanguard left the Clyde with 16 Trident missiles aboard that the Prime Minister got to hear about it.

Immediately he summoned Vincent Earlham from the Ministry of Defence and demanded: "Is this true?" Earlham, who knew nothing about it, could only stare back at him and say: "I've no idea."

Confirmation came soon enough. Tattersall's Private Secretary entered without knocking to report that the dockyard at Barrow were asking when to expect the fourth submarine.

"Stall them," said Tattersall. "Tell them it's been delayed or diverted or something - but stall them. "

Earlham opened his mouth but then waited until the secretary left. Finally, he said: "What are you doing? Are you trying to keep this quiet?"

"Of course I'm keeping it quiet. A submarine that goes missing with enough missiles to destroy a good proportion of the globe is not the sort of thing that ought to get out."

Earlham shook his head as if that would make sense of the idea. "But surely this is just what we need. This proves once and for all that the military are totally out of control."

The Prime Minister looked up at him with a mixture of contempt and pity. "Think about it Vincent - who let them get out of control? Us - we're responsible. We've got to keep this quiet and we've got to get that submarine back. I'm going to handle this myself."

He began to make phone calls, doing the obvious things while he tried to think of something that would actually do some good.

*

Susan Lomas tried again to telephone her father-in-law but succeeded only in bringing Mrs Morley to an even higher pitch of worry and excitement. The housekeeper had now, apparently, started to throw away good food because there was no-one to eat it.

"I'm very disappointed in Sir Charles," she said as if he was a little boy who hadn't come home for tea.

Susan listened patiently, knowing better than to try and interrupt. Finally she was able to get in a few words of sympathy and suggest that there must be some most exceptional reason why her father-in-law would treat anyone - let alone Mrs Morley (for whom he had the highest regard) - in such an inconsiderate fashion.

There was a sniff on the other end of the line and the housekeeper said: "That's as maybe... " and Susan was able to put down the phone with a smile.

Then she tried to relay this latest lack of information to

Peter. Now he was sleeping on the submarine they tried to phone each other most days. The first surprise was when she phoned his usual number at Faslane. The Wren secretary said: "Oh no, Mrs Lomas. you won't get him here. They all went off yesterday - to Barrow-in-Furness. Vickers dockyard. I expect he'll still be there."

She knew what that meant. She phoned the dockyard and got through to the manager's office. The secretary told her briskly: "All enquiries regarding Naval personnel should be addressed to the Ministry of Defence."

Susan frowned. Like any service wife. she knew better than to ring the Ministry. Instead she rang Faslane again and asked for a certain Lieutenant Commander who Peter had served with in fleet submarines and who had been a friend of the family ever since. He was guarded and almost monosyllabic.

She pressed on: "I can't find Peter anywhere and no-one will tell me what's going on. Everyone says I should ring the Ministry."

There was silence on the line for a while and finally the Lieutenant Commander said: "Look, officially nobody knows anything. But I'd say Vanguard's going to be away for quite a time."

"What do you mean? He's gone to sea? I thought they weren't allowed to anymore."

"Yes, well this is rather different."

"Why is it different? What's going on?"

The young man was now beginning to get embarrassed:

"Honestly Susan, I'm not supposed to talk about this at all. It's all very hush-hush. Just don't expect to see him for a while that's all."

Susan was becoming irritated by all this intrigue but clearly that was all she was going to learn about it. She said goodbye in the middle of a flurry of apologies. She put down the phone and went to the desk and got out the family-gram forms. The Navy realised that nuclear submarine crews needed some sort of news from home and allowed a weekly personal message of up to 40 words. Susan had become used to compressing everything she needed to say into those 40 boxes on the sheet. Carefully she printed:

"LOMAS, COMMANDER. YOUR FATHER STILL MISSING. MRS MORLEY BECOMING DISTRAUGHT BUT WILL SORT HER OUT. GATHER GRAPEVINEWISE YOU'LL BE AWAY SOME TIME. DONT WORRY WILL LOOK AFTER EVERYTHING. COME BACK SOONEST."

She still had nine words left and nothing much to say with them. She could afford to unscramble "GRAPEVINEWISE" but she was rather proud of that one and Peter would like it. So she added: "CLARE IN SCHOOL PLAY. LOVE YOU KISS KISS SUSAN."

Then she sealed the envelope and sat frowning over it.

*

"The fact is that we never dreamed someone like you

would come along, Prime Minister. It really never occurred to us."

It had never occurred to Mike Tattersall that he would one day have to rely on the likes of Professor Limpkin.

The Professor had spent the first half of his career designing nuclear weapons and now thought all that could be conveniently forgotten because he had seen the light and was now spending the second half advising the Peace Movement on how to get rid of them.

The Professor waved his coffee spoon in the air and went on: "We thought the great danger we had to guard against was the Dr Strangelove Syndrome - there was a film about it, you know. We feared someone in a position of trust would go mad and try to launch a nuclear attack. We built all sorts of safeguards into the system - special keys, matching codes, that sort of thing. We made it impossible for anyone to order a launch without the proper authorisation.

"But what we failed to think about was the possibility of someone on the inside trying to stop an attack. That was all down to the security people - all that positive vetting...

"So the result," he went on hurriedly, "The result is that the whole land-based firing system can be put out of action by one man with access to the right equipment."

He sat there smiling at Tattersall and nodding approval at his own cleverness. After a few moments he remembered to put down the coffee spoon.

Tattersall leaned across the desk and said one word:

"How"?"

"How? Yes how. Quite right." For a moment the Professor seemed to have lost his thread, as if an awkward student in the front row had asked the wrong question. Finally he struggled on: "Well, it's really very simple: There are two computers involved. One on the submarine and one at Fleet Headquarters. They both have the same program of random numbers and for any day between now and the year 2025 they will come up with the same sequence. Nothing can predict what that sequence will be - nothing, that is, except the other computer. "

"And..." Tattersall prompted him.

"And if the land-based program were destroyed, the submarine would not be able to confirm a launch order."

For the first time Mike Tattersall sat back in his chair and waited to see if the Professor found anything else to say. For once he didn't.

*

Dorothy Dean had been interviewed more times than she cared to remember. Her picture had appeared in just about every newspaper and magazine in the country and a few more across the world as well. There had even been a television documentary about her life. But she still distrusted the press.

That was why she preferred to think of Jamie Ferguson as a friend rather than a journalist. She knew she could trust

Jamie. Of course, she knew quite well that the cheerful young Scotsman made a good living out of selling stories about the Peace Camp to the national papers - that was how he had been able to set himself up as a freelance in the first place.

But at the same time, she knew that he would never misquote her and never write anything without coming to her first. And when the women wanted publicity - like the time they cut their way into the base and danced round the armaments depot ... Jamie saw to it that the photograph went round the world.

It was a comfortable arrangement and when Jamie arrived to record the women's reaction to the submarines leaving, she was all ready to fulfil her part of the bargain. She gave him one of those memorable quotes that newspapers could never resist. She told him: "Today we're all a little safer than we were yesterday –and tomorrow we're going to be safer still. Life's getting better at last."

Oh, she wouldn't be going home yet, she told him, not while the missiles were still in storage just down the road. The battle wouldn't be won until they had been destroyed completely and the base closed.

And then she drew him to one side. away from the other women and said: "There's something else. You know there were two submarines which had missiles on board?"

"Well, we assume they did."

She nodded patiently: "Only one came up here to unload."

"Perhaps we were wrong. Perhaps there was only one

that had missiles."

"Then why after I phoned London and told them, did the Head of the Research Department, no less, phone back today and tell me not to talk to anyone about it?"

She watched him working out the possibilities. He didn't seem to reach a conclusion. She said: "Don't make a big thing about it, Jamie. Just a word in the right place. Don't tell anyone where you got it from."

*

Elizabeth Crichton hardly thought about it anymore. The man who called himself Zimmermann had been right: Taking papers home had become second nature to her - as instinctive as remembering her handbag. She tucked the copies inside her blouse or - if there were a great many of them - inside the lining of her coat which she had carefully unpicked at the armhole. From time to time the bored security man on the door looked in her bag and she gave him a big smile and wished him goodnight.

And every few days the phone would ring late at night and she would talk to Lorenz for a while - never more than a minute or two.

And most of all, she followed the news - willing this disarmament business to be finished because when it was done Zimmermann wouldn't need her any more - and he wouldn't need Lorenz.

On the day the Government announced that the

submarines had left Faslane she worked in a daze - it was really happening. She copied long lists of nuclear shells and depth bombs going to the atomic research establishment at Aldermaston to be made safe.

She copied a document about submarines. It was a request from Number Ten Downing Street for all files relating to HMS Vanguard.

She wondered why No 10 should want those.

NINE

Bernie Price had the tip-off from the Strathclyde correspondent in front of him on his desk and he had the Ministry of Defence press office on the phone - and he couldn't reconcile the two.

The man on the phone had just repeated the statement which had been issued through the Press Association four hours ago: that three Trident class submarines had arrived at Vickers Shipyard, Barrow in Furness and the fourth, HMS Vanguard, had been ordered to a separate location because the yard did not have covered facilities for all four.

Price said: "What I asked you was 'How many of the submarines had missiles aboard when they left Faslane and how many unloaded them at Coulport on the way?'"

The man on the other end said: "I have read you the statement, Mr Price - and that is all that's being released at the moment. A press facility will be arranged to see the work in due course."

"Well, will you tell me where this "separate location" is?" But the Press Officer merely referred him back to the statement. Finally, with a theatrical sigh, Price asked him a question he could answer. He asked for the order in which the submarines had left Faslane and asked for the names of the captains. The Press Officer was only too pleased to tell him. He knew very well how reporters had to fill in with "colour" when they were short of facts.

What he did not know was that Bernie Price only wrote

down the name of the last submarine to leave - and he drew a ring around the name of its captain.

Price thanked the press officer with studied politeness and then pulled his keyboard towards him and tapped into the library file with: "P. Lomas."

Every P. Lomas in the library leapt onto the screen with a brief description. This was the way everyone who ever got into the pages of any of Britain's newspapers ended up being preserved forever. The Prime Minister was in there simply as "politician" and John Lennon was "singer" with "DEAD" inserted next to his name. The system was invariably demonstrated to visitors by showing them the file on the Loch Ness Monster. It was catalogued twice under "reptile" and "mythical creature" so as to cater for all points of view".

There were about a hundred P Lomas's. Everything from Acrobat to Youth Worker. There was no sailor or naval officer. Price frowned. He tapped out just "Lomas" and the words

"sailor", "navy" and "naval".

There was a pause while the computer searched. Then suddenly a single entry flashed onto the screen: "Lomas. Sir Charles. Kt. Naval Officer. It didn't look promising. Nobody knighted submarine commanders. Price tapped the "execute" and a list of headlines from each story ever written about Sir Charles Lomas began to scroll down the screen. Headlines were of course a notoriously bad guide to the actual content of the story. That was one area where the old system with an envelope full of cuttings stored in a filing cabinet had scored over the computer.

Price began to read his way through the file. The stories, cut from the original papers and laser scanned into the computer flashed on the screen one after another. This wasn't the right man at all. Apart from anything else he was retired. Still. it might be a start. Since he was a knight, he would be in Who's Who.

The phone was answered by one of those women who seem unsure that the instrument will work properly unless they shout. Price had to hold it away from his ear. This was Sir Charles Lomas' home he was calling. Commander Lomas lived up in Scotland. Yes, she did have an address for him. It would be in the book in front of her on the hall table. He waited while she searched and wrote carefully as she spelled it out to him as if it was somehow difficult: Craigmor House, Garelochhead, Strathclyde, Scotland.

Price got off the phone with profuse thanks for her help. Then he pulled out an atlas and found the place. It figured - the Commander lived just down the road from the submarine base at Faslane. Price sat and thought about it for a moment or two. Then he picked up the phone and booked himself on the next morning's shuttle to Glasgow.

The house did not look welcoming. It was exactly like the dozen others grouped around it, solid and grey. Grey stone walls and grey slate roof - the sort of imposing family house that a successful Scottish businessman might build for himself. But for all that, Price decided, the Commander had found himself a pleasant enough spot. The view down into the little bay with its boats bobbing in the sunshine would make up for a lot. He pulled at the old-fashioned bell.

The first reaction was the sound of large dogs barking; the noise echoing through the house. Then a very striking young woman opened the door. She had short blonde hair which made her eyes seem bigger than they were. She wore well cut corduroy trousers and a chunky sweater with a broad leather belt. Price was impressed. Somewhat tentatively, he asked: "Mrs Lomas?"

She nodded, understandably wary of strangers. "My name is Price. I'm calling about your husband. May I come in for a moment?" She invited him in readily.

As she showed him through the hall, she asked: "Are you from the base?"

By the time he told her "No", and gave her his card, he was sitting beside a framed photograph of Commander Peter Lomas, leaving her standing in front of him, fingering the card and evidently wondering how she was going to get rid of him.

She was too late.

He explained: "We've supported the Navy all the way through this and we plan to go on supporting them. That's why I need your help. I need to get in touch with your husband urgently. He's not at Faslane nor at Barrow. Can you tell me where to reach him?"

But instead she said: "How did you find me?"

"Well, your father-in-law... "

"My father-in-law; you've seen him?"

She sounded excited. Price tried to grasp the significance. He said: "No, I spoke to his housekeeper, but does that make a difference?"

Mrs Lomas just looked at him: "Why Peter, particularly. Why not any of the others?" He had no choice then. He had to tell her about Vanguard apparently, going to sea with a full complement of missiles - he had to explain about the Ministry's mysterious "separate location". The way he saw it, if he explained to her that something was wrong, she would have to help him – if only for her husband's sake. He even threw in his interview with the Chief of the Defence Staff.

But her face betrayed no clues. He didn't even know whether she had the slightest idea what he was talking about. She just said: "I'm sorry. I can't help you. I must ask you to leave."

He tried to persuade her. He argued with her and he even detected the first traces of a whine creeping into his voice. But in the end he knew she was not the kind of woman to be pushed into talking. He said goodbye to her with the distinct impression that something very odd was going on.

He drove the hire car back along the coast road until he saw a pub and treated himself to a single malt which he took to the telephone. He reversed the charges to the office and asked for the newsdesk: "Anything from Barrow?"

"Not a line. At least, not what you want. They've got a massive security operation on, claiming it's because they're not fully geared up to coping with nuclear reactors again. We've got correspondents checking all the other Navy dockyards we can think of - but nothing yet."

"Well I'm not filing this Vanguard line on what I've got so far. I'll be in the office later."

The news editor was not entirely happy with that. He had included Price's exclusive story on the news schedule and now had the job of explaining to the editor that it wouldn't be coming after all.

Price found that entirely satisfactory. He had never claimed it was anything more than a rumour in the first place. But that still didn't mean he wasn't going to move Heaven and earth to prove it was true.

*

Every morning at eleven O'clock they came to collect Sir Charles for his walk. A walk every day was what he demanded, and a walk was what he got.

It was the high spot of his day. The grounds of the old house were really quite beautiful and a gardener he never saw had planted begonias. He didn't even mind the guard who sat on a bench reading his newspaper and occasionally looking up to make sure his charge had not run off.

Sir Charles was not allowed newspapers, but no-one seemed to mind him reading the headlines as he passed.

This time he came to an abrupt halt. Right across the front page were the words "Nuke Subs Scrapped".

Very gently he said: "Excuse me. but may I see that?"

The guard was not sure. He looked about him and hesitated. Sir Charles went on: "If the Trident submarines are being scrapped. then surely I'll be released... "

The man chuckled: "All right then. here you are - but I never gave it you, right?"

Sir Charles smiled and nodded as if he made these kind of deals every day. He devoured the story in the space of a minute or two. It was frustratingly short. But it did contain one sentence that made him stop and grip the paper so that the page creased between his fingers:

The fourth submarine, HMS Vanguard, was ordered to a secret base until it can take its turn at the scrapyard.

The guard was clearing his throat and holding out his hand. Sir Charles pushed the paper at him and walked on.

What secret destination? Vanguard could be kept at Vickers wharf while waiting to go into the covered dry dock. The explanation was ludicrous to anyone who understood the situation. There was only one conclusion - one obvious, marvellous conclusion: Peter had taken Vanguard to sea. He had gone ahead and done this wild, crazy thing. The boy had done it!

It took Sir Charles almost 24 hours to get to see Carling - and he could understand why. The detective wouldn't even look him in the eye. He just mumbled: "I'm sorry, sir. I have my orders. You're to stay here until further notice. "

He didn't want to talk about the Prime Minister's promise or Habeas Corpus. He just trotted out the worst excuse in the world: "I'm only following orders".

In the end the Admiral turned and stared out of the barred window which at least gave him the. moral victory of forcing Carling to knock for the door to be opened and then slink away as if he'd been dismissed.

But at the end of the day it was Sir Charles who was looking at the world through 20mm steel bars. He took hold of them and began to pull. He could see the sinews of his wrists standing out against the wrinkled skin, feel the blood rushing to his face. He stopped and leaned his head against the metal.

That was when he admitted he was an old man. He stood there for a long time with his forehead against the bars, calming himself and forcing his brain to think logically. Whatever Tattersall's reasoning for keeping him locked up. he felt sure it was not just pure bloody mindedness. Clearly this old man who tried to pull steel bars out of solid concrete could still be a threat if he were allowed to go free.

Which gave this old man the mischievous notion that it was high time he was free.

He turned and looked around the room. Then he picked up a heavy plastic ashtray and began tapping softly at the wall, working his way along it, listening for a hollow sound...

*

The Prime Minister was being charming. It was something he was very good at. He sat his visitor down in one of the leather armchairs, he made a great show of pouring drinks - and of course he apologised several times.

By the time Mike Tattersall had finished with him. the young Ministry of Defence scientific officer would have completely forgotten about being hustled into a car by two detectives without so much as a word of explanation.

It was all very carefully planned - as it had been from the moment Tattersall read Gordon Cook's personal security file and discovered that not only did he work as a computer engineer at the Navy's fleet headquarters but that he was also classed as a category C security risk.

Quite simply, Gordon Cook was a man out of his depth. He had a second mortgage on his house and a steadily rising overdraft at the bank. He was exactly the man Tattersall had been looking for.

Now he sat there sipping at his lager, growing more at ease very minute and telling the Prime Minister what he needed to know.

"I never bothered too much with politics," he said. "I never reckoned my vote was going to make much difference. I suppose if I had to decide one way or the other, I'd be on your side - I'd go for nuclear disarmament. The only trouble is, my job depends on Trident... "

And very gently, Tattersall went to work on him. He jokingly pointed out that Cook's job seemed only too safe since the Navy were refusing to dismantle the Trident launch system - and then, almost as if the thought had suddenly occurred to him, he added: "Of course, you could come and work for me... "

Cook didn't seem to be sure that he had heard correctly. Tattersall went on: "I can't pretend there will be much job security - in fact you would be paid on results only. But if you could destroy the Trident launch code program, it would be worth £1million to the Government."

The young man stared at him. Tattersall put it another way: "If you do this for me, I will see that £1million is paid into a Swiss bank account in your name."

For a moment or two Cook was unable to say anything at all. He was one of those people who dream of £1million every week when they fill in their football pools. He was having trouble accepting it as a reality. Finally, he took refuge in something he knew. He said: "I can't do it."

Tattersall waited for him.

"What I mean sir, is that it's not possible. I mean the whole place is riddled with safeguards against that sort of thing. The computer will reject any program that interferes with its function and if I start disconnecting wires it sets up a whole barrage of alarms. If I disconnect the alarms, there are more alarms and apart from anything else, there are two back-ups on every circuit."

But Tattersall was not interested. He got to his feet: "I don't expect you to be able to tell me how you'll do it right away. But I'm sure you'll think of something. Detective

Inspector Carling will help you."

He was being confident because confidence is infectious. Very slowly, almost as if he was in a daze, the young man got up out of his chair and smiled.

*

It was a small hole, barely 30 cms by 50, cut in the ceiling with a table knife. Sir Charles Lomas had been forced hurriedly to eat two cold meals because of this hole. It was hidden inside the wardrobe and by taking down the hat shelf and putting a chair underneath, he could just squeeze himself into the attic.

The darkness, even after the dark of his room, seemed so intense that he couldn't imagine being able to move about at all. But first by feeling his way and then half imagining he could see the faint outlines of the timbers, he began to walk gingerly across the joists.

He came first to the water pipes running from the tank. It was a while, groping about in the dust, before he found the electricity cables. Mostly they disappeared down into the attic floor but he had a reasonable idea where he should be looking. The floodlight on the roof was above and a little to one side of his window - and sure enough there, where the roof sloped down just above the eaves, was a metal bracket and a cable running through a hole in the felt. Beneath it, through a gap where small birds got in, he could see the drive outside brilliantly lit.

From his pocket he took an old and rusty screw and began gently scraping at the plastic covering of one of the wires. When he felt the thread grate on copper, he started on the other wire. Within two or three minutes he had bared a small patch on both the positive and negative cables. Then he wrapped the head of the screw in a wad of toilet paper and, somewhat nervously, touched it across the two bare wires.

There was a big yellow spark and a loud pop and Sir Charles, dazzled and startled in spite of himself, snatched his hand away.

He peered through the birds' hole and could see nothing. All the lights on this side of the house had fused. There were shouts outside and the sound of a slamming door. As quickly as he could without stumbling in the dark, he started back.

For a moment, panic seized him when he couldn't find the hole in the dark. He should have trailed a string behind him like a potholer. In the end he almost fell straight down it.

A minute later he was in bed, back under the covers, eyes tight shut and heart thumping. He could still hear men shouting and the hurried tread of someone coming up the stairs without caring who they woke up.

The door burst open and a torch shone in. Sir Charles sat up, genuinely dazzled. The torch went out. The door slammed again and the key turned in the lock.

The old man lay back on his pillows feeling childishly

pleased with himself.

*

SYNOPSIS

Meeting of the Politburo of the Central Committee of the Communist Party of the Soviet Union. May 29th 1999. Item 1 (special projects).

Comrade the Chief of Staff of the Red Army. Presented the proposals for a conventional thrust into Western Europe (Appendix A). He stressed, however. the need to confirm beyond doubt that the destruction of the European nuclear weapons had reached a point where they could no longer be brought back into service. Comrade the Chief of Staff advised the committee that it would be unwise in the extreme to proceed with the programme unless that assurance could be given.

Comrade the Director of State Security reported on the progress of British nuclear disarmament. (Transcript paragraphs 76-86):

We have information that despite announcements from London, the British appear to be engaged in a deception regarding the disposal of their nuclear weapons. Satellite surveillance shows that on the day the Trident class submarines were said to have sailed from their base to be broken up, one appeared to return to its patrol.

The submarine, HMS Vanguard, carries a full complement of Trident missiles and is now believed to be on station in the North Atlantic.

The KGB Bureau of Planning and Strategy has compiled a report (Appendix B) offering various possible reasons for such a deception. Two of them deserve consideration by this meeting.

1. That the submarine has been sent back on patrol by the naval chiefs of staff against the orders of the Government. This would be a logical extension of the military's well-known dissatisfaction with the proposals of the Peace Movement, but it does not explain the Government's silence.

2. That the British wish to gauge the response of the Soviet Union to a nuclear-free Europe before committing themselves irrevocably to unilateral disarmament.

This seems the most likely. It would explain the British Government's silence, since not only would an announcement defeat the object of the exercise, but the action would undoubtedly be unpopular with their supporters. This theory also explains why the Royal Navy agreed to the three other submarines being broken up - a trial period of apparent unilateral disarmament may well be the price of the Navy's co-operation.

Since we do not know how long this "trial period" is to last, it would seem that any military intervention in Western Europe must be postponed indefinitely.

There would appear to be only two other options:

A. We furnish proof of this deception to the British press. The ensuing outcry among followers of the Peace

Movement would force the Government to recall the submarine and have it scrapped immediately.

B. We sink the submarine with our own ships and aircraft."

Comrade the Chairman discussed the options and concluded that to allow the British Peace Movement to lose face by exposing their deception would be counter-productive. He preferred instead to call on the Soviet armed forces to seek out and destroy the submarine.

Resolution:
It was resolved that plans for a conventional strike into Western Europe should be finalised but remain dependant on the destruction of the remaining British Trident class submarine.

TEN

It was the early hours of the morning and the lights throughout Vanguard were switched to red. That was all there was to tell the watch keepers that on the surface, night had fallen.

In the control room the seamen ratings on the steering and hydroplanes talked quietly as they stared ahead at their instruments, the control columns moving occasionally under the guidance of the autopilot. Throughout the submarine's 170 metre length, the few wakeful members of her crew kept Vanguard cruising at four knots and 50 metres. And that was all they knew. In Trident submarines nobody questioned even which ocean they were in.

But the Captain knew. In the Navigation centre, watching the green blip on the plot move a fraction of an centimetre as the system updated, he was working out how long it would take to get back to the U.K.

The whole enterprise had hinged on making some arrangement to supply Vanguard at sea. The normal patrol period was 60 days. He could go for twice that if needs be - more, if he started rationing. The trouble was that he had no idea whether he could expect supplies. Not one of the several messages from Fleet HQ had given the slightest hint that anything was being done - and another family-gram from Susan, still with no news about his father, worried him even more.

It was beginning to look very much as though he was on

his own. The decision was going to be his alone - and the fact that he didn't have to take it for another three or even four weeks did not make things any easier. He went out into the control room and nodded to the Officer of the Watch and then made his way back to his cabin. He didn't know it at the time but the Able Seaman walking down the passageway towards him was carrying the answer to a good many of his problems.

"Message on the broadcast. sir."

Lomas took it and stood reading while the man waited. It was from the Commander-in-Chief. Submarines Eastern Atlantic. LAND BASED FIRING SYSTEM NOW PERMANENTLY INOPERABLE. HM GOVERNMENT CONFIRM NO ACTION TO BE TAKEN AGAINST CAPTAIN OR CREW PROVIDING YOU RETURN BARROW IMMEDIATE.

There followed an urgent request for a reply. Lomas dismissed the signaller and went along to his cabin, sliding the door closed behind him. The one and most obvious item the message did not contain was a direct order to return. The C-in-C was leaving it entirely up to him. That was fine - except now there didn't seem to be any point in whatever he did because he no longer had any means of verifying a launch order - and in that case a launch would be unthinkable. Vanguard was all but useless.

He sat at his desk reading through the signal again as if somehow he could wring more meaning from it. Meanwhile there was one thing he had to do - he had to inform his Trident Systems Officer.

Lieutenant Commander Paul Evans was asleep at the time but saw nothing odd about being roused. All the same Lomas ordered coffee for both of them. The TSO, in shirtsleeves and with his hair freshly combed, was sitting in the Captain's cabin by the time it arrived. He read the signal and said: "Permanently inoperable, Sir? What do they mean?"

Lomas took the paper back: "I suppose it's possible that the Admiralty may have taken the system out of commission - yet why would they do that when they haven't once given us a direct order to return? It doesn't make sense. Still, we know one thing; there'll be no code verification on a firing message. Would you launch without that?"

It was a vital question. The missiles could not be launched without the permission of both the Captain and the Trident Systems Officer. Evans shook his head: "No sir, I wouldn't. Not the way things are at the moment."

"Nor would I. That's settled then - we've got to find out what the hell's going on." He dismissed Evans, and went back to the navigation centre. Ten minutes later Vanguard was on her way, at a tentative six knots, back to the U.K.

Lomas picked Sennen Cove for the landing-place because it had deep water close to a beach, a railway station within reasonable distance - and still gave him a clear run out into the Atlantic if anything went wrong. He picked Wilder to go ashore because this was official business - it wouldn't be right to send a junior officer.

Lomas swung the periscope, taking bearings: "Longships is that." The bearing-ring reader sang out: "Green 151."

"Pendeen is that."

"Green 050."

"Seven Stones is that."

"Red 098."

The pilot's pencil raced across the large scale chart: "1.9 miles to the drop point. Bearing 089."

"Down periscope. Course 089."

They ran on with the sonar and the depth recorder showing them the way until Lomas checked another set of bearings and ordered "Surface. Blow main ballast."

The high-pressure air wailed through the pipes and men scrambled into the tower. Lomas circled again with the periscope. He could see the water rolling off the bow, sparkling in the flash of the lighthouses: "Open the upper lid. Start the blower. "

Vanguard lay quietly in the slack water as the inflatable boat was manhandled out of the embarkation hatch and inflated. Within five minutes the deck party had the outboard motor shipped and three men scrambled down the curve of the casing. Lomas stood on the cramped bridge watching through night glasses as the dinghy set off at a quarter throttle to the beach. He waved but Wilder didn't look back.

*

It was well past dawn before Matthew Wilder saw a car on the road and stuck out his thumb. He didn't look exactly respectable in jeans and an anorak and he was surprised when it stopped. He had a story all ready, about his own car breaking down - but the driver wasn't interested. It seemed the bus service in the toe of Cornwall was so appalling that plenty of people regularly hitch-hiked to work.

He breakfasted at the station buffet and caught the 7.l4 which stopped at Slough. There he got a taxi and by lunchtime was walking up the path of a little Queen Anne house at Windsor. A motherly sort of woman in a floral housecoat came to the door. She said nothing but looked at him suspiciously. She was evidently not used to receiving callers who wore jeans.

He asked her: "Is Admiral Lomas at home?"

It was clear from her expression that she was going to be unhelpful but then a tall, grey-haired man appeared in the hall behind her. Wilder said: "Admiral Lomas?"

"Admiral Lomas is not here at the moment. Maybe I can help you. "

"My name's Wilder. It's a personal matter. Can you tell me where I'd find the Admiral?" There was a spark of recognition in the man's face and he came forward to the door. Whoever he was, the woman treated him with the greatest respect. In no time at all they were sitting in chintz armchairs in front of the French windows and the older man had introduced himself simply as "Harries".

He said: "You didn't really expect to find Sir Charles, did you?" Then he smiled and added: "I would guess that you are a Naval officer, Mr Wilder. While I cannot take you to Sir Charles, I can take you to a friend of his who may be able to help you. Will you allow me to do that?"

Somewhere in the back of Wilder's mind was a nagging thought that he ought to know more but on the other hand this tall and dignified man possessed an easy authority. It seemed natural to allow him to take over.

Harries had an expensive estate car parked considerately a little way down the lane and they drove slowly back into Windsor making polite conversation. Wilder did not immediately notice when they turned off the road and started down what appeared to be a private drive between two broad and immaculate lawns. He looked ahead to a huge stone archway and said stupidly: "This is Windsor Castle."

"It is. The Henry VIII gate." Mr Harries nodded to the policeman who took one look at his face and waved them through. He parked in a numbered space and led the way under a small arch and into the building via an ancient, iron-bound door. Wilder, too astonished to question anything, followed without a word.

They walked along lino-covered corridors and emerged suddenly onto the landing of a gigantic oak staircase. All around the walls were massive paintings and vases of flowers stood on every table. Finally, they stopped in a large sitting room, formally furnished and hung with paintings which even Wilder recognised. He was told to wait and spent five minutes inspecting two Turners and another that might have been Dutch.

Then Mr Harries came back and said: "The King has asked to see you. I have explained that you are not suitably dressed but he asks you not to worry. Please follow me. "

They set off again. This time along a gallery with more pictures down one wall and windows along the other. They stopped and knocked at a door and Wilder found himself being announced by his rank - he had no idea the man knew it.

The King got up from his desk and came forward with his hand outstretched: "Lieutenant Commander, it's a pleasure to see you - and a great relief as well."

Wilder could only mumble: "Thank you sir." He was vaguely aware of the other man leaving quietly and then the King was offering him a drink and sitting him down on the sofa. It didn't seem right that the King should fix his own drinks, but he did - a Perrier water for himself and a gin for Wilder. Then he said: "I want you to tell me everything that has happened."

That gave Wilder a jolt. He was quite well aware that the King was a Navy man. But he was also aware that it was "His Majesty's Government" that was trying to do away with Vanguard. The question was; which aspect of the monarchy was he dealing with?

But the King said gently: "Just start at the beginning

Lieutenant Commander. "

And he did. The King sat quietly and listened to it all. He seemed to take it very calmly. It was hard to tell whether or not he approved of what the Captain had done. In the end he nodded carefully and said: "What are your orders now, Lieutenant Commander? How do you get back to your submarine?"

"I'm to report to Admiral Lomas for fresh orders, Sir. The Captain's given me a week and after that he'll be watching for me every night where he landed me."

The King became businesslike then: "Leave that to me. I'll have everything ready for you in five days time. Meanwhile I want you to get right away. Take a little holiday where no-one knows you."

And Wilder, hardly able to believe what was happening to him, found himself shaking hands with the King a second time.

*

"Here's another one."

The man with the headphones spoke no louder than he would have done without them - but then he was used to wearing headphones. His companion adjusted his own and plugged a lead into the switchboard in front of him. The first man mouthed the words: "It's the fellow from the badminton club again."

"He was round there last Tuesday. You'd think she'd get

them mixed up."

The two men in headphones had a £1 bet on whether the wife of Vanguard's Petty Officer Cook would take her lover up to the bedroom or have him on the hearthrug. It was important because there was no telephone in the bedroom and it was the telephone mouthpiece which picked up the voices and relayed them down the Defence Communications Network which runs alongside the British Telecom lines to the drab office block opposite Chelsea Barracks in London.

But tonight the cook's wife chose to pick a fight with the man from the badminton club and after an entertaining few minutes argument he slammed out of the house. The cook's wife was then heard sniffling to herself and the two men in headphones called it quits and went back to work.

Most of the work at "Tinkerbell" - the telephone tapping facility inside British Telecom's Equipment Development Centre - was done for them by an American made computer nicknamed "Harvest" which could monitor 100 lines on each of its recorders. Two of these had been devoted entirely to the Vanguard operation.

Where possible the telephones had also been changed to a "live" mode which meant they not only fed the recorders with phone conversations but also everything else that was said in the room. It would not have been possible without the computer because "Harvest" was programmed to recognise key words and only alert the operators when one of them activated the system. The key words for the

Helensburgh number of the Submarine's Executive Officer were "Vanguard", "the boat", "Matthew" and "Matt". Whichever word it was that triggered the computer, it did not appear on the preliminary automatic transcription.

That began: "When did you get back?"

"Last night. Came in over the beach just like the marines. No-one's supposed to know I'm here. You mustn't tell a soul but we're on patrol again. I just came back to get a few things sorted out."

"You're not AWOL are you, darling?"

"Don't be silly, of course not. It's all absolutely genuine. It goes right to the top - I couldn't even tell you about that. Anyway, I've got to lie low for a few days while they sort out a problem with the launch system. We could go up to the Highlands, stay in a pub. If we left tonight no-one would have a chance to see me. "

"What? Now?"

"Well not exactly now..."

"Matthew Wilder, what are you thinking of."

The man reading the transcript as it came out of the printer picked up the jackplug which hung from his headset, jammed it into a socket and started dialling.

There was only one house in the road still with a light in an upstairs window. The black van coasted silently down the slight gradient and stopped right outside.

The two men who got out and closed the doors quietly

were dressed in dark blue boiler suits and black rubber soled shoes. Each carried a police issue truncheon and they darted straight into the dark passageway between the house and the garage. Then they took up positions on either side of the back door and waited without moving for ten minutes.

Finally, one of them hissed between his teeth. The other looked at him and the first jerked his head back towards the house. As if on cue the kitchen light came on. The back door rattled and there was the sound of an old mortice key turning in the lock.

As Lieutenant Commander Wilder emerged from his home, car keys in hand, the first man swung him off balance and the second hit him smartly above and behind the ear with his truncheon. Even as Wilder slumped forward the first man bent in front of him, swung the limp body across his back and walked fast back to the van.

The second man waited by the door. There was still the wife - and they'd been through this enough times to know how it should be done...

*

Pam Wilder was pushing the last of her toilet things into the corners of the suitcase when she heard it; a brief shout and then a scuffling sound. She stiffened and stood frowning, listening intently. Then she relaxed and smiled to herself. She needn't worry any more. Matt was home.

She hoped he was all right. She wanted to call down the stairs and shout "Darling, are you all right?" but she really mustn't be so silly. It was all very well being nervous when he was away - he expected that - but it irritated him if she fussed too much when he was home. She put it out of her mind and went round the bedroom tidying her possessions. She wouldn't be back for almost a week and she liked to leave things just so.

When there was nothing left to tidy, she had zipped up the suitcase and Matt still wasn't back. She began to worry in earnest. Now she thought about it, she hadn't heard the car starting up. She stood in the middle of the room and allowed the panic to take hold of her. The complete silence of the house was unbearable, closing in around her in a way neither her husband nor the surgeon commander who gave her Valium could understand. She felt her face flush and she was breathing hard. She went to the top of the stairs and called down - silence.

She put her foot on the stair and then rushed back into the bedroom and scrabbled in the bedside drawer for the Pocket Cop. Matt had brought it back from America for her. He'd pretended it was a joke, but he probably suspected that when he was away, she carried it clutched damply in her hand on these night time searches through the house. It was only as big as a fountain pen, but the instructions said that when you pressed the button it would direct a powerful jet of tear gas into the face of an assailant. She held it in front of her like a talisman.

She knew every corner where a burglar could hide. Countless times she had leapt into the spare room pointing her Pocket Cop foolishly at the lamp behind the door. But it gave her confidence. She worked her way methodically through the house calling softly: "Matt, are you there?" Until finally she came to the kitchen.

The back door was open. She stared at it. Her searches through the house had always stopped at the back door when she put her hands gratefully on the two heavy bolts Matt had fitted and turned the key as far as it would go. But now it was open. She was whimpering quietly but she took a deep breath and then she launched herself through the doorway. At the last moment, she remembered the garage wall and turned so that she hit it with her shoulder.

And there was the burglar coming at her just as she had always known he would, dressed all in black and with a black hat and evil eyes shining in the darkness. She screamed and as she went on screaming, she pressed the little red button with all her might.

Somewhere, it seemed very far away, there was a hissing sound and a deep yell of surprise and the man seemed propelled backwards against the kitchen window, clutching at his face. He swore and struck out with his short black stick, yet his other hand was pushed hard against his eyes.

She could smell the gas now - stinging her nostrils. It seemed to act like a trigger to her senses. Dropping the still-spluttering aerosol. she began to run - not into the street but back towards the garden and the enclosed world she knew.

She almost ran into the clothes drier in the dark. One foot sank into the earth of a flowerbed, but she didn't stop until she ducked behind the garden shed, and stood panting against it with her head thrown back and stared at the stars. Then she looked back the way she had come.

There were two men. She could see them clearly in the loom of the street lamps, between the dark shapes of the house and the garage. One of them broke away and came loping across the garden. He was coming for her. She felt she couldn't take this. She couldn't cope. Sobbing uncontrollably, hardly knowing what she was doing, she began to climb onto the pile of old paving stones left over from the path. She jumped down into the Jackson's garden next door. They had taken down some of the fence between their garden and the one behind it so the two families' children could run back and forth. From there she got out into Queen Street and then along to the main road - a small frantic figure running blindly with tears streaming down her face.

ELEVEN

"While they sort out a problem with the launch system.."

Tattersall played the tape over and over again and it still agreed with the transcript - but that didn't mean it made sense.

He wished Carling could have stayed and discussed it. He had a lot of time for the quiet. efficient policeman. But Carling had to go and deal with Wilder. There was nothing to do but play the tape and wait for Limpkin to be brought up from the country.

When the Professor finally arrived, he was tousled and angry and began to protest in a ghastly whine which Tattersall cut short. saying: "Listen to this."

Then he played the tape once more, adding: "That's the second-in-command of the submarine Vanguard. He's back to "sort out" the launch system - except you and I know (and he should know) that the launch code program has been destroyed. He can't sort out anything at all. That submarine is impotent - so what does he think he's up to?"

The little man looked harassed, frightened even. Tattersall should be a little kinder, perhaps...

But he was tired and he was worried. He went on: "What can he do for Christ's sake"?

Limpkin blinked twice and licked his lips: "Perhaps he's come to arrange some other sort of code." The Prime Minister actually banged his fist on the desk: "But that won't work, will it, because the computer on the submarine won't recognise any code except the one produced by the computer at fleet headquarters. That's been destroyed so the missiles can't be launched - so what's he here for?

"Of course the missiles can be launched."

Tattersall stared at him. For a long moment there was complete silence between them.

The missiles can still be launched?"

"Oh yes. "

"Even without the code being verified by the computer on the submarine?"

"Certainly. "

"Explain."

An expression of awful realisation swept across Limpkin's face. He said: "I'm sorry if you're under a misapprehension but the system was designed only to prevent an unauthorised order being transmitted. Obviously, the submarine must always be able to launch its missiles - no matter what might have happened ashore.

"I mean even if the headquarters and all the means of communications were destroyed, it was still essential that the enemy should know that nothing whatever could stop the retaliation. That was the whole philosophy behind the deterrent you see. There was supposed to be no way of stopping it."

Tattersall said: "I didn't know this."

"It was never a secret. But with all the public discussion about the sophisticated measures built into the system to prevent an accident, I suppose no-one saw any point in alarming the public by explaining it."

Tattersall could hardly believe what he was hearing. He had no doubt there were people who knew more about the subject than he did - he'd dealt with the moral rather than the practical side of disarmament. Now it seemed he was about to ruin everything by ignoring the basics.

"You mean this Captain - this Commander Lomas - has the power to destroy a quarter of the globe just like that? What if he goes mad or something?"

"Well he wouldn't would he. They're all given the most rigorous psychological tests and anyway he couldn't do it without the co-operation of his officers."

The way the professor explained it was not quite as frightening as the idea of a man in his late-thirties roaming the oceans with his finger on the button - but it was not far off that. If the Captain and crew were convinced they had a genuine order to launch a nuclear attack, then they could do it.

They didn't need computers or a code which changed every day. They could manage with a few figures scrawled on a piece of paper. That was why Wilder was here. He had come to pick up a piece of paper...

*

Susan Lomas answered the phone before she had properly woken up. It was a long time before she made any sense of what she heard. There was someone talking about burglars and kidnapping. Finally, she shouted down the phone: "Who is this?"

The jabbering stopped abruptly and then, with an almost pathetic urgency the voice went on: "Susan, it's me - Pam. Please, please help me. We've been attacked and they've kidnapped Matt. He said it was all secret and no-one was supposed to know he's back and, so I can't tell the police or the base or anyone. I don't know where to go or what to do and you were the only one I could think of... "

It was all coming out so fast and half of it didn't make any sense at all. Susan got out of bed and pulled on her dressing gown. She could think more clearly standing up. It was the way anyone would expect Pam Wilder to behave. She had always been quite unable to cope with any kind of a crisis - and it was always Susan she turned to first. It would help, of course, if she had a child. Very slowly and carefully Susan made her read out the address on the phone box and told her to stay there. Then she stood quietly for a moment or two holding the phone and thinking. This would happen at half term. It was just as well her mother was staying. She wouldn't have wanted to go out in the middle of the night without a babysitter...

She still had the phone in her hand, the dialling tone purring softly. As she went to put it back the note changed. It was almost as if someone had been listening on the extension. She frowned. Then she dressed quickly, scribbled a note which she propped it on the kitchen table and got the car out. On the way, driving round the side of the loch with that slightly unreal sensation that comes from country roads at night, it occurred to her that there had been a lot of unexplained happenings in her life lately. She shook herself out of it. Pam Wilder was probably exaggerating again.

Pam was not exaggerating. One look at her torn clothes and the scratches on her arms was enough. Susan said: "You'd better stay with me tonight. Whatever it is we'll talk about it in the morning. "

But of course Pam couldn't stop talking. She rambled on about Matthew appearing on the doorstep, about some sort of secret mission and then a holiday in the Highlands - about him disappearing and burglars at the kitchen door. And as she told her confused and disjointed story, Susan drove more and more slowly until finally she pulled up just outside Garelochhead.

"What's the matter?" said Pam.

"How soon did this happen? How soon after Matthew arrived?"

"I don't know. Two hours, perhaps."

"Have you noticed anything funny about your telephone?"

"The telephone? "

"A sort of echo - as if there's someone listening in?"

"No..."

"But you phoned me didn't you. I don't think we will go home. "

She drove to Glasgow Airport's Holiday Inn where she took two adjoining rooms and Pam Wilder fretted about not having her sleeping pills. Susan opened the fridge in the corner and poured them two miniatures of gin. Then she put the Executive Officer's wife to bed almost as if she were a baby.

She poured another gin for herself in her own room and sat on the edge of the bed drinking it slowly. She wouldn't be able to sleep anyway, not after what she'd heard. Everything fell into place now. If Peter was on patrol again instead of waiting to take Vanguard to the breakers yard, then it was small wonder no-one wanted to tell her what was going on. It might also explain what had happened to her father-in-law: For all she knew he might have been kidnapped just like Matthew Wilder.

Wherever she thought of turning for help, she would be turning to the authorities in one form or another - to the very people Peter was hiding from. There seemed to be no-one outside that world who could help her - no-one else who knew anything about it.

And then she stopped. There *was* someone. There was one person who seemed to know an awful lot. There was the man from the newspaper...

He'd given her his card but she'd thrown that in the wastepaper basket straight away. She put down her glass and called directory enquiries for the number. It seemed to ring for ages. Even at four in the morning she imagined there would be people at work in a newspaper office. In the films newspapermen never got up before lunch and rushed to work at midnight. When the number did answer she found she couldn't remember the man's name.

"I want to talk to your defence reporter. It's urgent."

The switchboard operator was silent for a moment or two and then repeated slowly: "You want to talk to the defence reporter. "

"Yes, I'm afraid I can't remember his name but he came to see me and I wouldn't talk to him then. But now I want to very much."

The operator said slowly: "I see."

As he said it she realised that newspapers must be rung up in the middle of the night by countless lunatics, insomniacs and people who can't get on radio phone-in programmes.

She took a deep breath and started again: "Please, I'm not trying to waste your time. This is a genuine call."

The man seemed to sigh and said: "Putting you through."

Again she had to wait. With no ringing note. she thought she had been cut off. But finally, a sleepy and bored voice said: "Newsdesk."

She was more careful this time; "My name is Susan Lomas and your defence reporter came to see me the other day. I'm afraid at the time I was not able to talk to him. But now something has happened that makes it most important that I do talk to him as soon as possible."

"Our defence correspondent is Bernard Price. Is that who

you mean."

"I think so. He was sort of middle-aged and quite small. He had a hat."

The voice on the line became fractionally more interested: "That's Bernie. But he's not here now, you know. It's four in the morning."

"Please... "

The man hesitated and finally said: "All. right then. I'll ring him but if he doesn't want to call you back until the morning don't start ringing me again, O.K?"

She promised and gave him her number and then she got into bed and waited.

*

Bernie Price had made his decision. He was going to ring her in the morning. He lay with his eyes closed, perfectly comfortable and about to go back to sleep.

Except he was still awake.

He had no idea how long he stayed like that but in the end, he hoisted himself up, grumbled hugely and hunted about on the bedside table for the number. As soon as she answered he knew the worst: Mrs Lomas wanted to make a deal.

"I believe you know something about HMS Vanguard and I need your help but I want you to promise me you won't put anything about it in the newspaper."

Very slowly he said: "I'm sorry, I don't make those kinds

of promises."

He lay back while she wittered on, saying how important it was and how he could write it later but not now. He listened to her for a bit and then, as he found himself more awake he cut in: "Look you've woken me up at in the middle of the night to ask me to help you. Certainly I'll help you but I don't make deals so why don't you sort out your problem, whatever it is, by yourself - and leave me to get some sleep."

For good measure, he made the gesture of putting down the phone - except of course, he didn't. Instead he hung on and waited and after a moment or two she said: "Are you still there?" and he said: "I'm still here."

He knew he'd won then. She wheedled a bit more but Bernie just lay there listening to her chattering on and waited for her to get round to telling him what all this was about. When she did he stuck a foot out of bed and hooked the chair towards him so that he could reach the notebook in the jacket pocket. He took a more or less verbatim note of everything she said after that.

By the time she finished he had reached two conclusions: One was that if this was true then he was listening to the biggest newspaper story of the decade and the other was that the story was not in Susan Lomas at all, but the other woman Pam Wilder.

Two minutes later he had a firm date to meet them both in the Holiday Inn at Glasgow Airport. Then he rolled over and went straight back to sleep. He was troubled only slightly be a small twinge of conscience.

*

The correct name for the lie detector used by the British security services is the Polygraph and the only thing Matthew Wilder knew about it was that there were ways of fooling it. Combat crews in the RAF were trained in resisting it. There were things like Yoga and self-hypnosis. He knew just enough to realise, as a pressure belt was passed round his chest and a blood pressure cuff went on his wrist, that he was about to tell these people everything they wanted to know.

Somehow it would have been more bearable if they had tied his hands behind his back and punched and kicked him. That was what he had expected when they brought him to the large, secluded country house somewhere near London. But a Polygraph ... it was so clinical, so certain.

The technician attached the wires and switched on. The paper began to crawl out of the machine.

"What is your name?"

He knew it would start that way. This was the "control" question. He looked at the technician, at the other men standing around, watching him carefully. Suddenly it dawned on him that if he said nothing at all, the whole exercise would become pointless. They would have no way of knowing what was the truth and what was a lie.

He thought of telling them they would get nothing out of

him - that was what people did in the films - but perhaps the machine would be able to read something even into that. So he sat there perfectly still and said nothing. He did not, for fear of betraying himself, look any of them in the eye.

"What is your name?"

Say nothing. He could sense them watching, feel the questioning glances across the room. He stared at the wall. Say nothing. What is your name? A pause and then a voice said "wait" and one of the men and the technician left the room. It seemed they were gone a long time and the silence burned in Wilder's ears. But he never looked at the others. He felt a wild sense of excitement. He had cracked it. They couldn't do a thing. They had all this equipment and they were powerless as long as he kept his mouth shut. But then the one who seemed to be in charge came back and pulled up a chair and sat in front of him and said: "Lieutenant Commander, there seem to be one or two things you don't understand about this machine so we're going to give you a demonstration. We're going to tell you your collar size - now you might not think that's a matter of national importance and you'd be right. But all the same, you must admit, it's not something we're likely to know. Now, is it size 16?"

The technician didn't take his eyes from the graph paper for a moment. Then he said: "No." Wilder began to feel uncomfortable. The man went on: "Is it size $15^1/_2$?" He could feel the flush rising to his face. He must think of something else, concentrate the mind. Think of the boat - no, that was no good - think of home...

The technician said: "No."

"Is it size 15?"

Think of Pam. Think of the holiday in the Highlands. Oh God. "Yes." The technician almost shouted it.

The man in front of Wilder got up and casually walked round and pulled back the neck of his shirt: "Polyester cotton, made in the U.K. Size 15. Well, there you are, that wasn't very difficult was it? Now let's try something else."

He sat down again. so close this time that it was impossible for Wilder to avoid staring into his face. In a gentle, conversational tone. the man asked: "When you rejoin your submarine back over the beach like the marines, I think you said will it be in... Scotland?"

The voice of the technician seemed to come from very far away: "No."

"Will it be in...Wales?"

"No."

"Will it be in... South West England?"

There was a pause then. The technician wasn't sure. Wilder felt a surge of excitement, but his mind was being dragged back from where he wanted to focus it.

The technician said: "Yes. "

After that he knew it was hopeless. If he'd had the training he could have managed. He was sure he could. He was so nearly there but the answers came out almost as surely as if he'd given them himself - which he supposed was what it amounted to anyway. The time and place of the pick-up, the recognition signal. They got them all. He sat slumped in the chair, almost weeping with frustration.

———————

TRIDENT

TWELVE

The car showed no sign of leaving - and anyway, what about the half dozen slates he had so carefully removed from the roof? He had no idea how to put them back.

Sir Charles got up and dressed a second time.

Once again he shut himself awkwardly in the wardrobe and clambered up into the attic. An irregular patch of dimmest grey showed where the slates were missing. He moved across the joists, feeling his way from memory. He was acclimatised - just as the guards were acclimatised to the problems they had suddenly begun to have with the floodlights. He could even put his hand instantly on the screw wrapped in its piece of toilet paper.

No longer did he flinch at the spark but immediately started counting. Last time it had taken them two-and-a-half minutes to mend the fuse. He planned to be well past the trees by then.

There was a piece of flex tied round one of the roof timbers - it was the only piece of his equipment he couldn't find instantly. He held onto it and pushed his legs through the hole, throwing out the rest of the coil behind him. He heard it slap agonisingly against a window.

He had stopped counting. He forced himself to breath easily and began to climb down the wall. He'd been taught to do this the proper way years ago by the Marines. It had been easier then. The wire kept catching on his clothes. He arrived on the ground breathing hard and feeling slightly dizzy.

He looked both ways like a child about to cross the road and then walked quickly across the drive. The gravel crunched under his feet like a succession of pistol shots. When he reached the grass he began to run, realising suddenly that it must have been years since he had run. He felt exhilarated. He supposed that he must be drunk on adrenalin.

The sky was beginning to lighten and now he could see his way between the avenues of rhododendrons. He had no clear idea of the layout of the gardens but as long as he kept the house behind him he had to find the wall.

When he did, coming suddenly on it around the corner of a hedge, he stopped dead - now feeling very old. The wall was three or four metres high and the undergrowth had been ruthlessly cut back from it so there was nothing to help him scramble up. Even if he managed to, there were "Y" brackets on top with six strands of barbed wire angled out on both sides. He fought down a bout of panic and set out at a jog trot to the left. If the only way out was through the gates, then that was the way he would have to go...

The gates were as high as the wall and they were closed. To one side was a little wooden summer house where a man sat drinking tea and reading a paperback. Sir Charles had never seen him before. He ducked round the hedge out of sight.

A minute later he emerged clutching a stone the size of a child's fist and walked over to the summer house. He rattled the door and shouted through the glass: "One of them's got away." It was the first thing that came into his head.

The guard laboriously unlocked the door. As soon as it swung back, Sir Charles brought up his fist and hit the point of the protruding chin as hard as he could. With the stone still clutched in his hand, the force was considerable, and he could feel his knuckles protest. But the other man went down. His knees buckled, and he keeled over backwards, knocking his tea to the floor as he went.

Sir Charles stood over him for a moment or two, massaging his hand and flexing his fingers.

As far as he could tell nothing was broken. He worked steadily then, yanking the cord from the telephone to tie the guard and binding a handkerchief tightly across his mouth.

Then he turned to the panel on the desk. There were several switches for the alarm system and one for the gates. He heard a faint clank as the electric bolt drew back in its housing and then the two rubber tyres began to turn, dragging the big iron gates slowly open.

It took him a moment or two to realise he had done it - that he was out. And then he was running, sprinting down the road with the long strides of a young man.

*

It was some time before Matthew Wilder realised what was happening. The questions had stopped and there was a commotion in the house, the sound of people running and shouting orders. The man who seemed to be in charge went to the door and spoke urgently to someone outside. Then he turned and said: "Lock him up. We'll go on with this later."

Wilder allowed himself to be lifted to his feet and half pushed out of the room. They took him upstairs to a small bedroom with a single barred window. It occurred to him to ask what was going on but he said nothing. He stood in the centre of the room and heard the key turn in the lock and gave himself up to despair.

"We'll go on with this later," they had said - and he knew what the next question would be. He could almost hear the quiet conversational voice: "Now we're going to find out who you've been to see since you've been back - who it is behind all this."

Did they already have a suspicion? Would they go through a list of names - politicians, senior officers?

Perhaps they would read through the Navy List. Would it contain that particular name?

But he was clutching at straws and he knew it. There wasn't any hope. There was, in fact, only one way out. Wearily he began to look around the room: A built in wardrobe, a dressing table, one rather old fashioned armchair. He wandered into the bathroom and saw the shower head fixed solidly to the wall above the bath...

He would need some rope. There was a pull cord for the light but that wouldn't be strong enough. He went back into the bedroom, irritated that it should be so difficult. The flex for the bedside light might do. He tried to pull it out of the lamp but it wouldn't come so he took the whole thing with him into the bathroom. He stood on the edge of the bath and tied a clove hitch over the shower head so that the lamp hung down level with his head. In the other end of the flex he made a timber hitch and, with one hand against the wall to steady himself, slipped it over his head.

He stood there for a few moments looking around the bright, modern bathroom and suddenly caught sight of himself in the mirror. He found it odd that he hadn't realised there were tears running down his face.

*

Bernie Price was polite, he was understanding - and he was hard at work.

First he got the two women out of the Holiday Inn and registered under false names at a rather luxurious country house hotel 15 miles away. He also organised a photographer to fly up from London.

Someone else was busy collecting films from a wedding photographer on the south coast because they couldn't risk going back to the Wilder house for pictures of Matthew - and the only problem he had left was a nagging uncertainty about basing the whole story on the word of one highly emotional woman.

He went through it with her in every detail and he had no

doubt that it was true - but he was still going to have to write it in terms of Mrs Wilder's claims rather than bald facts. He didn't like it but he had no choice.

In the afternoon the women went shopping for clothes. The photographer, a rather vulgar Cockney called Dave Channon went along as "minder" and to pay the bills - and Price settled down in his room, picked up the phone and dialled the direct number for the Ministry of Defence press office. He said: "I've just been speaking to the wife of the Captain of HMS Vanguard and also the wife of the Executive Officer... "

He paused to gauge the effect he was having. As far as he could tell there was only polite interest. He went on: "They told me that the submarine is at this moment on patrol and not about to be broken up at all."

The press officer was silent for a moment and then said: "Are you sure?"

"That's what they told me."

"Sounds extraordinary. Look I'll have to check this."

Price waited half an hour and called back - and then another half an hour. In fact it was almost two hours later that he found himself talking to the Ministry's head of information services, a new man appointed by Earlham himself. The head of information services said: "Mr Price, I don't know where you're getting this from... "

Price told him.

The man said: "Are you sure?

Price said he was. Eventually he began to get irritated:

"Do you know where HMS Vanguard is or don't you? Because one way or another I'm going to write this and it's going to look rather odd if you haven't got an answer."

The head of information services didn't like his tone: "We have never released Vanguard's exact whereabouts for security reasons - you know that. But she is in dockyard hands and waiting to be broken up.

"Have you seen her?"

"Well no, not personally..."

"Has anyone?"

"Look I don't know what you're getting at Mr Price..."

"You know perfectly well what I'm getting at. I've made half a dozen official requests to visit this mysterious dockyard but neither I nor any other journalist has been allowed near the place."

The head of information services began to bluster: A facility would be arranged... the information was classified... surely Mr Price would understand...

Price was beginning to understand only too well. He changed tack: "And Mrs Wilder's claims about her husband being kidnapped?"

"They will be investigated."

"That's all?"

"Yes, that's all."

Price thanked him heavily and put down the phone. Then he got out his computer and, with his notes beside him on the dressing table, began to write.

He pitched it as hard as he could but every so often that

awful phrase kept creeping in: "It was claimed yesterday". He tried saying: "According to Mrs Wilder" but when he got to the end, he knew it wasn't as strong as it could be. He read it through twice, entered it in the memory and called the office.

With a confidence he didn't entirely feel he said: "B. Price here. I have a merry tale of seafaring folk for you. If you will put me on, then I will deliver."

The man on the desk waited for him to finish his little ritual and put him through. The hum of the computer came back down the line and Price fitted the phone into the acoustic coupler. Then he called up the story and the machine fed it down the line.

He went back on to the desk and this time found himself talking to the news editor who came straight out and said: "Bernie, we've got a problem with your nuclear submarine stuff."

"You can't have, I've only just filed it."

"Well, one of the chairman's cronies has heard about it and he's raising merry hell." Price began to feel very cold inside.

Back in the hotel lounge, he found Channon incongruously presiding over the tea table. Price pinned on a smile and said: "We have a problem. I have to go back to London. I'm afraid I must ask you to stay here with Dave."

They all started asking questions at once and he went on: "The chairman has taken an interest. Apparently, he has a friend - astonishing as it may seem - and this friend somehow knows what we're up to. He's started making a nuisance of himself."

It was a moment or two before he realised Susan Lomas was saying: "My father-in-law."

"I beg your pardon?"

"Peter's father. I've been trying to get hold of him for ages. I told his housekeeper she could reach me through your office."

Price stared at her. She went on brightly: "He knows all sorts of people. It would be just like him to ring up your chairman. I'd better come with you."

Price wasn't happy about the idea. He came up with half a dozen perfectly good reasons for Mrs Lomas staying. But she just smiled at him and said: "Well I've decided I'm going to London. You can come with me if you like. Pam will be perfectly fine here with Mr Channon."

Price was beginning to build up a healthy dislike for Mrs Lomas, but he knew when not to argue - all the same, they must have looked an odd couple setting out together in frosty silence.

On the plane, they had a brief discussion on the topic of Mrs Lomas' father-in-law and Price decided he was beginning to dislike the whole family. He felt relieved when they got to the office and he could leave her in the interview room with a cup of coffee and go in to see the editor.

There was no coffee here. George Snelling ran his

newspaper on the high energy principle: If the man at the top wasn't seen to stop for an instant, then no-one else could either. He had Price's copy up on his screen. He said: "If this is true, it may well be the most important story you or I ever handle. If it's not true, we're going to look idiots and the powers that be are going to crucify us. What happens if this Mrs Wilder turns out to be a looney?" Price didn't have to say anything. They both knew the story's shortcomings. The editor went on: "We might just have found another source to verify it - this friend of the chairman." He tossed a buff envelope of the man's clippings onto the front of the desk.

Price glanced once at the name and said: "Father of the submarine captain. "

By the time they were summoned to the Chairman's office, the editor was convinced and ready to fight for the story.

The aged secretary announced them and there, sitting to one side of the great desk and smiling with perfect defiance, sat Susan Lomas. Price forced himself to smile and nod. He shook hands with the Admiral as the Chairman hurried through the introductions and got down to business.

"I have assured Sir Charles that he will be speaking entirely off the record - my personal assurance..."

Price had time to catch the full implication behind the Chairman's glance before the old Admiral cleared his throat and began to talk as if he was addressing a briefing: "I'm afraid Mr Price has stumbled on a matter of national security which cannot possibly be allowed to become public knowledge. " He was addressing himself to the editor - ignoring Price. He went on: "I will admit that much of what he has discovered is substantially correct but for reasons which I have outlined to your chairman, I regret I must ask you not to publish. I do apologise for the inconvenience. I should have explained things to my daughter-in-law. I blame myself entirely." He gave a little bow as if that was the end of the matter.

It wasn't. Price opened his mouth to protest but the editor beat him to it. George Snelling knew enough of his Chairman's secrets to question just about anything. He questioned this most forcefully: "I"ll accept that everyone knows any newspaper will do favours for its friends - we might ignore the odd divorce or plug a new restaurant on the diary page - but here we're talking about the most flagrant piece of public deception of modern times. I think we have a right to know by what authority Sir Charles is making these demands."

For the first time the old sailor looked slightly unsure of himself. He almost mumbled: "I can't tell you that. All I can say is that it comes from the highest authority."

Snelling leaned forwards and said: "Who?"

In his younger day, George Snelling was supposed to have been one of the most tenacious reporters the paper had ever known. Price was enjoying the demonstration: "You're asking me to drop the biggest story of the decade -

of the generation even - because someone somewhere who you won't name thinks it's not in the national interest. I'm sorry but if that's all you can offer me as a reason then the story runs."

The Chairman interrupted: "Now George, I've known Sir Charles for many years and I'm prepared to accept his word. It's my decision. I invited you and Mr Price here because I thought you had a right to know the reason.

"Yes, well we're not being told the reason, are we? This newspaper has a reputation to live up to - a reputation, incidentally, that will be worth precisely nothing if this ever leaks out."

Then, having raised the temperature of the meeting to his satisfaction, he turned to the Admiral and added: "Of course there is one other option. There's no doubt that the story we have at the moment is hardly complete - after all it's based on the word of one woman alone, that's if we accept that Sir Charles' comments are off the record."

Sir Charles looked startled and glanced at the Chairman for reassurance. Snelling went on: "No doubt the story will develop and ultimately there'll come a time when it will be public knowledge. If, when that time comes, we were to have an exclusive record of everything that had happened, then it might be argued we had delayed publication for sound journalistic reasons."

There was a long silence. Price thought the logic inescapable. Even the Chairman seemed to be thinking it over. Finally, he turned to Sir Charles and said: "I think that might make rather a good compromise - Mr Price will obviously be keeping track of the story anyway. If you agree to help him with that, then I will ensure that we don't run it until you say so - or until it appears in another paper, of course."

The negotiations went on for some minutes, but it was clear to Price that one way and another he was going to keep his story. He glanced across at Susan Lomas and was rewarded with a look of undisguised hostility. He smiled back encouragingly.

Finally, a sort of agreement was reached. Price would be kept up to date on developments while Sir Charles had the right to withhold the name of the man behind the whole business. He was fanatically insistent about that. Price had no doubt it would emerge in due course. Meanwhile, so that everyone knew where they stood, he produced a notebook and laid it ostentatiously on his knee.

Sir Charles, who had started to bring them up to date, paused and appealed silently to the Chairman. Then he sighed and went on.

Price could see how the whole business fitted together now. There was no doubt it was the most astonishing tale. As usual at times of great excitement. he found his shorthand suddenly became faultless.

Then Sir Charles paused and, speaking slowly for the first time, he said: "It seems likely that Lieutenant Commander Wilder has been arrested by the same people who held me prisoner. They made me take a lie detector test but because of the state of my health that was inconclusive. However, the Lieutenant Commander is a fit young man. We have to assume that by now the Government knows about the entire operation - including the fact that the submarine will be at the rendezvous in five days time."

THIRTEEN

Detective Inspector Donald Carling sat still and accepted the tirade without flinching. He had been bawled out by senior officers maybe half a dozen times in his career. He probably deserved it then and he certainly deserved it now - but nothing had prepared him for the vehemence levelled at him across the Prime Minister's desk.

It was loud, it was long, and it was extremely lucid. He was incompetent - that, he certainly accepted. He had been charged with a most important assignment and he had bungled it like a 19-year-old rookie just off the beat - that was true as well.

Worst of all, with half a dozen trained men at his disposal, he could not even contain one old man who should have been in a retirement home.

There was much more that he didn't even hear because, vicious as it was, it still meant less to him than his own feeling of failure. Maybe that was why he was able to keep his head clear and notice something that made him feel even more uneasy - the way the PM was taking Lieutenant Commander Wilder's death. Undoubtedly it smacked of the "suicides" in the cells of some miserable police state. But it wasn't the death itself which seemed to worry the Prime Minister. It was the fact that Carling had allowed it to happen before he had finished the interrogation.

The charge was not Murder but Inefficiency - and this from the man who had railed at him for slapping a couple of old Admirals around. Carling saw the warning signs and he noted them.

Gradually the flow diminished until Tattersall began to hunt around for his words. They sat there looking at each other, both knowing this was pointless - nothing more than a show of frustration. The Prime Minister swallowed hard and gathered his thoughts for a moment. Finally, he said: "So what about this rendezvous. What chance does it give us?"

And then they set to work. Tattersall refused to call in the Navy and Carling had to admit that no submarine captain would take much notice of his own side threatening to sink him unless he surrendered.

"We're going to have to pose that threat ourselves," he said. "We're going to have to find a way or sinking that thing if it doesn't do as it's told."

Tattersall shook his head: "We can't sink it. No matter what happens, it's got to stay afloat."

The detective raised an eyebrow. After dismissing Wilder's death, was the PM now becoming concerned for the rest of the crew?

Tattersall, totally calm now, began to explain: "You're forgetting something. That submarine has to be delivered to the dockyard. It's got to be seen to be dismantled. If you sink it, then how the devil are we going to disprove all these rumours - what's to stop anyone believing it's still out there on patrol? I want to see that submarine being broken up on television.

"I'm not interested in how you do it, Inspector - but I want it done."

Carling left soon after that. He could think of nothing else to say that was constructive and he wasn't going to condemn the idea as impossible until he'd had a chance to think about it.

He thought about it long and hard. He went for a walk in St James's Park, sat on the grass with his hands clasped around his knees - and it was only when he had covered every angle that he took a taxi to Old Street police station in the City.

They knew him there from the days when he used to draw firearms from the armoury. He said his hello's, shook a hand here and there - and made his way to a room at the back of the ground floor with a Perspex plate on the door which said: "Specialist Armourer Major I. C. Meake."

The room was filled with pipe smoke. On two sides were steel workbenches, one fitted with a lathe. At the far end a miniature firing range was banked up with sandbags for preliminary tests on the weapons. In a vice was what had once been a Uzi sub-machine pistol but was now fitted with a wooden stock and a thirty centimetre barrel. In the middle of it all stood Major Meake, a dirty white coat over his tweeds and an oxy-acetylene torch in his hand. He pushed up his goggles and produced a pair of half moon spectacles from is top pocket. He looked over the top of them and smiled: "Donald, come in, come in. "

Major Meake, once of the Royal Ordnance Corps, always

kept open house for his regulars and Carling, in his terrorist-hunting days, had been very much a regular.

The Major filled a blackened kettle, balanced it over the gas forge and pulled up two stools. "I thought," he said, relighting the pipe, "that you'd become respectable."

They sat there and chatted a while. The Major liked to chat. Then they drank tea and Carling said: "I want you to make me one of your toys - but it's not a normal job and I can't get you the usual authorisation."

The old engineer looked over the top of his glasses again: "Well I can't do anything without the right bits of paper, you know that."

"But I can't think of anyone else who could do the job and it's so hush-hush I'm not supposed to tell anyone about it. In fact I'm not supposed to tell you."

The Major chuckled: "Well then laddie, I'd say you were stuck. "

"Exactly, so I have to break a few rules and I want you to break them too. When you hear what it is, I think you'll find it quite a challenge."

Major Meake sucked up a mouthful of tea and sat staring into his mug for a long moment. He seemed to know better than to ask a lot of questions. He just sat and did a bit of weighing up for himself - and finally he held up an oily finger and said: "One condition. If I don't like it for any reason at all, I won't do it. But one way or another, I won't tell anyone."

Ten minutes later, they agreed that no-one would believe

him anyway.

*

Price sat in Clarinda's cockpit doing his best to keep out of the way. Dave Channon, on the opposite seat, was unusually subdued - he was also clearly terrified.

All around them sails flapped, winches screamed - and Price had the feeling that it was all being laid on to prove they hadn't known what they were letting themselves in for. The Admiral still refused to tell them where they were going and Mrs Lomas was embarrassed. She couldn't understand why they insisted on coming along. She seemed to think they should be content to be told about it afterwards.

The boom swung uncomfortably close and then the Admiral undid the chain which held them and without a word, Mrs Lomas began to pull on another rope. Then there was another sail flapping. Channon held onto the side, his knuckles white and his face a mask of sheer fright.

And then suddenly everything quietened down. The sails filled, the boat leaned over and began to move. Mrs Lomas steered them between two other yachts, passing so close that Price could have reached out and touched them. Gradually he began to relax. They swept down the loch very fast. He realised they had the tide helping them. He could see the submarine base with two of the Fleet boats beside the quay. Something occurred to him: "Won't they see us?" he asked. "Won't they guess what we're doing?"

Mrs Lomas shook her head: "I take Clarinda out all the time while Peters' at sea - besides. I don't think they know one sailing boat from another. Even if they do, I hardly think anyone's going to raise the alarm."

She smiled then. It was the first time he had seen her smile. It might be that she was just enjoying sailing her boat but Price wasn't going to waste the moment: "Anything I can do?" he asked.

The Admiral. standing holding onto the rigging, glared at him - but Mrs Lomas seemed pleased. She said: "Thank you, Bernard. The genny needs to come in."

And so he learned to undo the rope from the cleat, fit the handle into the winch and, with Channon holding onto the tail of the rope, he wound in the sail until it stopped flapping and the boat pushed harder through the water, leaving two long trails of creamy white foam.

Price felt rather proud of himself. Mrs Lomas laughed. It was the first time any of them had laughed. She moved aside: "Come on. You steer."

Gingerly he took the tiller and at once the little yacht veered to one side, rocking madly. The Admiral staggered and sat down with a bump - and then Mrs Lomas put out her hand and brought them back on course: "You're over-correcting," she told him. "Everyone does that at first - you'll soon get the hang of it. "

And to his own amazement as much as anyone else's, he did. He steered them down the loch and out into the Clyde where the waves were bigger and a little spray blew back to wet them. Dave opened his mouth to say something and then thought better of it. He was beginning to look preoccupied.

Mrs Lomas went down into the cabin and came waving a little packet. "Anyone for a pill?" she asked brightly. Channon manfully said nothing. But then, when she popped one into her own mouth, he took the packet and helped himself.

Price felt fine. This was fun, but he didn't know how long it would last. He asked: "Should I have one too? I feel O.K. at the moment but I'm not terribly used to this,"

The Admiral spoke for the first time: "Don't take it yet. See how you get on. You may be one of the lucky ones but there's only one way to find out."

It occurred to Price that the old man might want to see him ill to prove he should never have come in the first place. But Sir Charles seemed to be genuinely interested. He might even be softening. Price decided to pull his weight - after all he might even be some use.

He steered all the way down the Firth of Clyde, past Bute and Cumbrae. They ate sandwiches and drank beer and the wind died a little and Channon cheered up enough to take his turn as helmsman - and so they made their way cheerfully, if a little erratically, out into the Irish Sea.

*

"If it doesn't work. I'll give you your money back." said Major Meake. "But I won't come and pick up the pieces."

Carling looked at the apparatus on the workbench. It certainly didn't look as if it would work. It looked like nothing he had ever seen before. There was a metal drum like a flat biscuit tin attached to two curved arms which fastened with something that looked like a complicated butterfly nut.

The armourer chuckled: "It's your own fault for making the job so difficult. Submarines were never designed to be disabled. They were designed to keep going or sink - no half measures. But this little fellow solves your problem. It only wrecks the propeller. He picked it up and began to explain: "A modern submarine doesn't have a propeller like a ship. A submarine's propeller has more blades but each one's thinner - that's to cut down on turbulence and make the sub quieter. Anyway, I have it on the very best authority that this will fit round them. "It's small so that it can sit there and not be noticed but it's powerful enough to blow the whole thing off its bearings or at least turn the blades into so much scrap metal. "

Carling nodded: "How do you detonate it?"

"Remote control. On land you'd use radio waves. Under water I've substituted sonic waves. The only trouble is that the ocean's full of noises of one sort or another and if I set this to the same wavelength as something we haven't considered like a dolphin's mating cry or whatever, then it might go off when you least expect it. So, you've got three signals, arranged like the combination lock on a safe."

He took a plastic box from a drawer. Carling recognised it as a standard issue police radio but with a coil of wire leading from one end to a small funnel shaped device.

Major Meake went on: "It's all right, there's more in here than a VHF transmitter - the casing was the right size, that's all."

He turned it over. On the bottom were three buttons coloured red white and blue: "You press each button in turn, that throws three contacts in the firing circuit. When the last one connects, up she goes."

He held up the funnel shaped object: "This is an underwater loudspeaker. You drop it in the water. These other wires connect to a l2 volt battery."

Carling took it from him and turned it over in his hands. The armourer added: "It works, I tried it in the serpentine. Range is probably a couple of miles, but you'd best stay closer than that. I could make it more with a bigger speaker, but you'd need more power for that. I'd think this would do."

Finally, Carling smiled: "Yes," he said. "I think it probably will."

*

The moon made a silver path across the water, a narrow, sparkling line which stretched all the way to the horizon - and Clarinda sailed straight down it.

Bernie Price sat in the cockpit in a state of supreme contentment. After a two-day crash course from Susan, he had learned enough about handling the little yacht to be allowed to stand a watch by himself. True, Sir Charles was dozing fully clothed on his bunk ready for any emergency. Ready, in fact, to come up and look around if there was so much as a change in the motion so Bernie was careful to keep the boat moving just as she was.

He had learned to feel the wind on his cheek and could tell if it shifted or the boat began to wander. He had also learned to steer by a star and had one swinging back and forth in the rigging. He knew that as the earth rotated, he would have to find another star, so from time to time he checked the compass.

One way and another Bernie Price decided there was something rather special about being alone out here with the boat slipping over a calm sea and the pale green light of the phosphorescence glowing in the wake. He began to hum a little tune to himself. He was interrupted by the alarm clock beeping softly in the cabin.

The dim shape of Sir Charles moved on the bunk and then he was standing in the companionway, looking around and sniffing the air.

He said: "There's the loom of Pendeen."

Sure enough, over the horizon on the port bow, there was a momentary glow, and then another. Sir Charles watched it, his lips moving as he counted to himself. Then it came again, and he said: "That's Pendeen all right. Group flashing four every 15 seconds."

Somehow Price was disappointed that he hadn't spotted it first. Sir Charles bobbed down again and lit the stove. Coffee at the change of the watch was a ritual and soon the smell of it wafted out into the night. Price took the mugs and set them on the leeward seat and then Sir Charles came out and took the helm. Price settled himself with his coffee on the other side. For a long time they sat in silence, listening to the occasional creaking of the gear and the steady rustle of the water along the sides. Then Sir Charles said: "You can go to sea all your life and still not tire of nights like this."

Price laughed easily then: "I thought it was just me. I've been sitting here fairly bursting with poetry." Then he added: "We're nearly there aren't we?"

"Oh yes, about ten or eleven O'clock in the morning. A bit too early really, but then we weren't to know we'd have a fair wind the whole way. Price hesitated, not wanting to spoil the moment. But he went on: "What are we going to do?"

"Do? Well, we're going to warn them off of course." And then the Admiral smiled one of those rare smiles which crinkled up his eyes and made him seem very human indeed: "I'm sorry I had to keep you in the dark but there's no harm in you knowing now. The fact is, if the Government know Vanguard's going to be here, then she hasn't got a chance. Once a submarine gives away her position in confined waters, she's even more vulnerable than a surface ship. Our job is to ensure she doesn't make the rendezvous.

"We can't risk trying to contact her through the Naval communications network. But we can be sure that if Peter sees his own boat when he checks the coast through his periscope, he'll know something's up. From there we shall have to play it by ear - for instance I still have to pass on his new orders. "

Price nodded: "Meanwhile we just go to Lands End and sail up and down. "

"Correct. We sail up and down and wait."

FOURTEEN

Carling lay with the chill of the damp sand seeping into him and thought it through once again. He'd been on enough stake-outs to know that you had to think of something to keep yourself alert and if you thought of the job in hand, there was less chance of it going wrong.

But no matter how much he thought about this one, he couldn't find a single flaw. He only had to play the part of Wilder long enough for the submarine's inflatable to get into the shallows. After that he could rely on his silenced Walther automatic.

He had a police frogman on the rocks over to the right ready to swim out with the mine and he had another to stay behind and operate the detonator in case the submarine tried to make a run for it.

Once the police launch from Falmouth arrived, the trap would be shut. On board was Major Meake with a second detonator. It would take him an hour and a half to get round from Newlyn but then he needed only to follow the submarine to the dockyard at Barrow, ready to blow its propeller apart at the first sign of trouble.

Carling was pleased with the plan. He told himself there was very little to go wrong - but he knew better than to believe it. He patted the sand to make a hollow for his chest and began to think it through once more.

*

Where the rocks marking the end of the cove plunged into three metres of water, Sergeant Benny Rutter sat uncomfortably in his wet suit. A compressed air cylinder was never intended to be worn for long periods out of water and he had to lean back against it, propping himself painfully against the granite.

He hadn't liked the job from the first. Looking for bodies in gravel pits was one thing. But being suddenly assigned to the Special Branch and then finding himself doing something like this - well, that was quite another.

But he kept his doubts to himself. The young P.C. with him seemed to look on the whole thing as a great adventure. He kept saying stupid things like: "It's just like being in the SAS" and playing with the detonator, checking the crocodile clips on the car battery at his side and fiddling with the wire that led down into the water at their feet.

Rutter imagined himself swimming out to the submarine with the mine strapped to his chest - and hoped the young man would have stopped fiddling by then. He had half a mind to let the lad do the job himself. But he was the senior man and he had old fashioned ideas about leading by example. He was beginning to regret that.

*

Peter Lomas could see the silver light of the quarter moon filtering down though the water before the periscope broke the surface. With the submarine stationary there was none of the usual disturbance. One moment there was just the opaque glow and the next, as the water drained off, the panorama of coast with the Longhop's light flashing to starboard.

He flicked on the image intensifier and walked the 'scope round the full circle. There was a sailing yacht making its way round to the north but otherwise no shipping in sight. He turned back to the coast and asked quietly: "Time?"

"Twenty-three fifty-eight, Sir."

He waited.

At first he almost overlooked the tiny winking pinprick of light. It was so dim it might have been a table lamp seen through curtains or the dynamo of an old man's bicycle. But as he watched, it continued to flash, slowly and deliberately short long short: The letter R.

Lomas waited to see it again and be sure. Then he said: "There he is. Course for the pick-up point please, Pilot."

"082 Sir," The navigator had already made his calculations.

"Steer 082, revolutions for four knots."

As the propeller began to bite Lomas could see the waves moving towards him, imperceptibly at first and then faster as Vanguard picked up speed. He kept her down for the time being, taking another sweep round as Evans alerted the shore party under the embarkation hatch. The little yacht was still pushing on to the north with the steady south easterly behind her. It was a good night for a passage. He turned back to the business in hand.

He took bearings on Pendeen and the Longships and then on the Seven Stones and adjusted the course to cope with the last of the ebb tide. As they came into position, he took her up. He didn't want to hang around any longer than he had to. The water ahead of him became confused as the high-pressure air emptied the main ballast tanks.

Then he swung himself onto the ladder and started climbing.

*

The two divers saw the submarine at the same moment and both pointed at once.

Immediately Carling's voice came from the radio: "Rutter?"

The Sergeant picked it up and thumbed the transmit button: "I see it sir. I'm going in now."

"You'll have to be quick. It's a long way out. I'll give you all the time I can." Then he added. apparently as an afterthought: "Good luck. "

Rutter didn't reply. He was spitting into his face mask and rinsing it in a rock pool at his side. He was going to have to swim much further than he had expected - half a mile, it looked like. Benny Rutter didn't like that. He liked things going according to plan. In police work, once you started adjusting the plan, problems began to creep in.

He settled the mask firmly over his face, checked the mine

strapped to his chest, put the mouthpiece between his teeth and, with the P.C. helping him, slid backwards into the water.

At first he swam on the surface to get his bearings and then dived to a metre - just deep enough to keep his feet under and stay below the wave motion. He kept the moon in the corner of his eye to give him a course and pushed forward with long, powerful strokes. The force of the water dragged at the mine hanging beneath him and breaking his streamlined shape. All the same, he was travelling fast. He surfaced a couple of times to check his progress - once about half way when he was going too far inshore and then again 200 metres from the submarine. He could hear it now. It made a noise like a cistern filling as water entered its ballast tanks and it began to sink deeper. At first he thought he was too late, that it was already on its way. Then he heard the rapid threshing of an outboard motor. That would be the inflatable going to the beach.

He came up against the hull of the submarine so fast he almost crashed into it. He turned and followed it to his right, keeping within arm's length.

He could see the rudder now, so tall that it stuck up like a sail. He thought of the photographs he'd seen and tried to work out how much further there was to go. The sheer size of the thing startled him. Then, splayed out like giant metallic leaves he saw the blades of the propeller. Each one was almost two metres long. And they were thinner than a normal ship's propeller blades. Rutter pressed himself against the one nearest the vertical and worked the two arms of the mine around behind it, feeling for the butterfly nut and the locking pin.

*

Peter Lomas watched the inflatable become swallowed up in the darkness near the beach. The outboard motor had been cut and the paddles were out.

He turned awkwardly on the tiny crowded bridge. One of the lookouts glanced at him and said: "All clear astern sir, excepting that yacht. It's turned round now, heading back to the south."

That was odd. Why would it want to turn back? A sailing yacht rounding Lands End in the middle of the night must be on her way somewhere. More to the point, she now had the tide against her. He looked through his binoculars. They were good night glasses, but he could see only the outline of a sail against the horizon - perhaps two miles away and close hauled on the port tack. He adjusted the focus a fraction and caught his breath. The yacht was reefed.

He looked up at the sky and turned his cheek to the wind. It was light, moderate at the most - no more than ten knots. There was only one reason anyone would reef a yacht in these conditions and that would be to slow her down. Who would deliberately slow down when they were punching a foul tide?

Lomas slipped rapidly down the ladders to the control room calling "Up search" as he emerged from the tower. He flicked on the image intensifier and swept round the seaward sector. The little yacht leapt out of the darkness at him, discoloured by the green of the instrument but as large as life. She had the first reef tied down and was carrying a working jib. She seemed to labour through the slight waves, ridiculously under-canvassed and probably only making two or three knots. She was an old boat. he could tell that by the box-like coachroof - rather like his own boat.

He could feel the sweat grease the rubber padding round the eyepiece as the truth hit him. This *was* his boat. There wasn't a yacht anywhere quite like Clarinda. He could even see the extra ventilator cowl - and as she lifted to a wave he saw, just for an instant, the name on the cockpit dodgers.

He did his thinking on the way up the tower: The only other person who sailed Clarinda was Susan and what would Susan be doing here - standing off and on - obviously waiting. Before his head was out of the hatch he was calling to the yeoman signaller: "There's a yacht bearing about Green 135. Make to her "Two Bravo Delta Victor - Kilo"

2BDV was Clarinda's radio call sign and "K" the international single letter code for "I wish to communicate with you".

The signaller took the Aldis lamp and clanked out the message. It took him no more than a few seconds. The light couldn't be seen from the land anyway.

The little yacht sailed on in darkness. Lomas said softly: "Again. " But even as the signaller lifted his lamp a light began to blink back at them. Two short, one long.

"Yacht makes: 'You are running into danger' Sir."

Lomas didn't need to be told. But what danger? They were clear of the rocks on each side of the bay. He looked at the coast where the inflatable was paddling invisibly towards Wilder on the beach. They were the ones in danger. He grabbed at the microphone: "Control: Bridge. Recall the shore party."

Then he looked around. Vanguard was still lying parallel with the shore. She ought to be facing out to sea. Underwater the submarine could turn with all the agility of a fighter aircraft, banking on her hydroplanes. But lying static on the surface she was about as manoeuvrable as an ocean liner. In fact, since she didn't have two propellers to thrust in opposite directions, she was less manoeuvrable.

The trick was a quick blast forward with the helm hard over to get the water moving over the surface of the rudder and then a similar run astern with opposite helm.

He spoke again into the microphone: "Control: Bridge. Starboard thirty."

*

Benny Rutter felt the movement of the water like a breath of wind as the rudder swung behind him.

Christ, the thing was going to start up.

The butterfly nut was tightened down now. He jammed the locking pin into it and the mine sat snugly against the upright blade of the propeller. Compared to the size of everything else, it looked insignificant.

Time to go. If someone had bothered to move the rudder, the chances were the prop would start turning any minute and he didn't want to be anywhere near it when it did. He began to paddle backwards with his hands, watching the blades all the time for that first, imperceptible movement.

But it didn't happen like that. One moment they were stationary with the moonlight filtering through them and the next they were almost a blur, turned on as instantly as an electric mixer.

The submarine of course, did not move at all to begin with - 16,000 tons deadweight does not accelerate like a speedboat. At first all that moves is the water around the propeller.

Benny Rutter was in that water. He watched the spinning blades grow larger in the frame of his facemask. He kicked frantically with his fins and paddled with his hands.

But he was sucked backwards and upside down for maybe three metres. He opened his mouth to scream and the regulator fell out - and mercifully, as he shot feet first into the vortex, he blacked out.

*

At first Carling thought it was a trick of the light. He went down to the water's edge, still flashing his torch. It gave him a different perspective but still the rubber boat seemed to have turned round.

Then the outboard motor started.

Instinctively he pulled out the pistol, but he'd never have the range with a silencer - and without one he'd give himself away.

Now he could see the white wake as the boat bounced over the waves - and beyond it, the dim shadow of the submarine. As he watched, the shape of the fin began to change. It was getting narrower. The submarine was turning, ready to go out to sea.

He fumbled for the radio: "Rutter?"

It was a moment or two before he got an answer. Then the young P.C. came on: "The Sarge isn't back yet, sir. He's been gone a good half an hour now sir and I haven't seen anything of him. "

The boy sounded worried. Carling dismissed it: "Detonate the mine. "

"Sir?"

"Set the mine off now. The sub's going out to sea again. If you don't set it off now the bloody thing will be out of range. "

"But what about the Sarge, sir?"

"Never mind him. Set it off now, d'you hear?"

There was no answer. The boy hadn't even pressed his transmit button. Carling continued to watch the submarine.

It was still moving slowly - presumably waiting for the rubber boat to catch up. But it was getting further away all the time. Carling waited for the explosion - a column of spray like an underground geyser, he imagined. But nothing happened. There was just the black shape of the fin cutting across the horizon and growing smaller all the time.

He lifted the radio again: "What's the delay?"

"No delay, sir." The boy's voice squawked with a falsetto that had nothing to do with the radio. He was just plain terrified: "What about Sergeant Rutter. sir. He's still in the water. If I let this thing off it'll kill him. He might not even have fixed it to the submarine at all. He might still be carrying it. I can't set it off, sir... I can't."

Carling swore once. Then he called up the police launch and gave it the order to move but he knew he was too late. It had to be the detonator on the rocks. Still clutching the radio in one hand, he began to run along the beach.

Even staying on the wet sand near the water's edge, it was hard going. The water sucked at his shoes, he couldn't see where he was putting his feet and tripped over lumps of seaweed. At the end, of course, he had to climb over rocks and through pools, banging his knees and scraping his knuckles. In all it couldn't have been more than 500 metres, but it took him an age. Meanwhile the submarine had picked up its boat and was steaming fast out to sea. Carling leapt the last stride to where the young constable stood holding the detonator, apparently in some sort of daze. Without a word Carling took it and pressed the three buttons - red, white, blue. Nothing happened. He tried again - more slowly this time, remembering about the three circuits which had to be completed before the electricity could reach the explosive. But the submarine was maybe three or four miles away by now. When he looked again he could no longer see it.

He stood there, breathing heavily. The young policeman was saying something to him. He forced himself to concentrate.

The young man said: "I'm sorry, sir."

FIFTEEN

"She's diving, now what do I do?"

Bernie Price held the tiller in both hands as Clarinda leapt over the waves with a full genoa while Sir Charles helped Susan shake out the reef and made the little yacht sail even faster.

They were still following the submarine, still pushing out into the Atlantic, but although Vanguard had seemed to settle lower in the water as she picked up speed, now she was definitely going underneath it. Soon all that remained above the surface was the top of the fin with the periscope and radar mast.

The Admiral looked up from untying a reef point: "She won't leave us, " he said. "Not while we're flying the K flag. She'll just stay submerged in daylight, that's all."

Price looked away from the last patch of broken water to the starboard crosstree where the blue and yellow signal flag blew straight out. Then he settled to steer by the compass again.

Channon moved over and sat beside him with his back to the foredeck, masking himself from the other two. "You realise, " he said. "That if that thing's only going to come up at night, I'm not going to get any pictures."

Price hadn't thought of that. He was becoming far too involved in sailing the boat. If he wasn't careful he'd forget why he was here.

Channon lowered his voice even more: "I'll go along with

you, Pricey - you're running the show. But you'd better fix it for that thing to come up in daylight or I'll be going home with two dozen rolls of unexposed film. It's all right for you, you can busk it but here I am on the biggest story since the eviction at the Garden of Eden and I've got sod all to show for it."

Price waved him into silence as the Admiral came clambering back to the cockpit. It was a tricky moment - but the old boy was feeling pleased with himself and that made him talkative. He sat on the lee side, his face redder than usual from the exertion. He said: "They're leading us out into the Atlantic. It's too crowded here with all the shipping coming down from the west coast ports. They'll surface again well away from the coast - probably tonight, under cover of darkness."

Channon's jaw tightened slightly but he had the sense not to argue. Instead he asked, quite reasonably: "How are they going to lead us anywhere when they're underwater. We haven't a clue where they're going."

The Admiral nodded. "Periscope," he said. "If we get off course, they'll show a periscope to put us right. They've got sonar to tell them where we are. We won't be lost, you'll see."

And they weren't. From time to time throughout the day. the mottled grey periscope rose from the water reminding them all instantly of the Loch Ness Monster. It was such an extraordinary sight it seemed only natural for Channon to produce a camera and pose Susan sitting on the cockpit coaming with the periscope staring back at her.

They sailed on steadily westwards. The mood was lighter now the job was almost done. They toasted each other in beer at lunchtime and then in the afternoon, took it in turns to get some rest as the excitement of the night before caught up with them.

Then, after sunset, as Dave Channon sat on the coachroof smoking quietly and watching the last of the light drain from the western sky, he spotted the periscope once more. They looked without much interest. The sight was a matter of routine now. But this time it rose far higher than usual. One moment it was three metres above the surface and then it began to look like a ridiculous stalk growing taller and taller out of its feather of white water. Another mast followed it and finally there was the long black top of the fin, pushing a great curling wave in front of it.

Ten minutes later a small inflatable came racing towards them. Susan saw her husband and waved excitedly and the man sitting in the middle raised his hand. Sir Charles brought Clarinda into the wind as the boat came alongside and then Commander Lomas, wearing a long black oilskin coat and a lifejacket, clambered aboard his yacht.

There was a kiss for his wife, he shook hands gratefully with his father and then turned to Price and Channon. Sir Charles made the introductions and even in the half light the Commander's anxiety was obvious.

Sir Charles was probably as close to embarrassment as he ever came: "Long story, " he said. "Rather complicated."

Then he ushered his son down into the cabin, turning to Susan as he went and saying pointedly: "Would you entertain our two friends from the press in the cockpit. Peter and I have some things to discuss in private."

Price stared at him and so did Susan. Under his breath, Dave Channon said something very rude.

*

Peter Lomas wanted first to kiss Susan in a way that was not really possible on a small boat with strangers aboard and second, he wanted to know what was going on. In the familiar, softly creaking cabin of Clarinda, he got at least one wish.

His father talked rapidly in what seemed very much like a prepared speech. He glossed over some parts of the story and when he came to his arrest and escape, Lomas had to concentrate hard to catch the details. He got the impression it was a considerable achievement for a man in his 60s. But when they came to Wilder's disappearance, he butted in, horrified. It had, after all, been his idea to send Matthew ashore. He felt responsible and his insides turned over at the thought of what might have happened.

"We'll have to get him back," he said, thinking immediately of the hard men from the Special Boat Service he used to carry in fleet submarines.

But the old man shook his head: "It's not important. Not in terms of the job to be done. Whatever he might have told them, he'll have told them by now. It's unfortunate but we have to carry on as if nothing's happened, do you understand?"

Lomas realised it was not merely his father sitting across the cabin. It was a senior officer. He nodded, and despite himself, he said: "Yes sir."

The old man grunted his approval, as if he had known this would be the hardest part. Then he went to the bookshelf above the chart table and took down a buff envelope. Inside it was another envelope in heavy, good quality paper and with an old-fashioned wax seal over the flap. It was addressed to Cmdr P.R.C.Lomas and marked "Secret". Lomas took it and turned it over in his hands. He looked across the cabin and raised an eyebrow.

His father went on: "That's your missile launch code. You will open it only to verify a firing order."

He paused. "Of course, the present government has not the slightest intention of giving firing orders. But circumstances change and so do governments. If the worst should happen then the Prime Minister of the day will be offered this code and it will be up to him to decide whether to pass it on to the Navy."

Lomas nodded. He wondered vaguely who was keeping the code, waiting for the day a Prime Minister might need it. He doubted, somehow that it would be his father and from what he had just heard, it wouldn't be a serving officer. He knew either way that it didn't concern him.

Meanwhile his father went on: "None of this is any good

at all unless a potential enemy knows that Britain still has nuclear weapons. We have to make sure the Russians take that into account. So, for once in your life you must arrange for the Soviet Navy to locate and identify Vanguard."

Lomas stared at him. This was one thing he had never expected. Hiding from the Soviets' scores of fleet submarines had become so much a part of his life that he found it almost impossible to imagine deliberately giving himself away. But he could see the logic. He took a deep breath and nodded. Then he said simply: "I think we can manage that."

*

The hard part had been persuading them to let him come along. It had never occurred to Price that now he was here, he wouldn't be allowed to talk to Commander Lomas.

The submarine captain sat in the dark of the cockpit and said: "I can't see what good it would do. I don't want to be famous."

Price told him: "You're going to be famous anyway. When this gets out, you're going to be on the front page of every newspaper in the country - and the point is that all anyone will know about you is that you disobeyed orders and became a sort of privateer, swanning around on your own with enough missiles to wipe out a quarter of the globe. How much do you think people are going to trust a navy whose officers behave like that?

"But if it's explained to them in terms they can understand. If they know something about the kind of decisions you've had to take, what kind of man you are, then maybe they'll look at it differently. Basically what they need to know is that you're not crazy."

Lomas didn't seem sure what to think. Price could see him gradually reaching the decision that senior officers always reached. He was about to say "No" because "No" never got anyone into trouble.

And then suddenly the Admiral interrupted. He said: "I think Mr Price is right." Price stared at him, trying to see his expression in the darkness. The old boy went on: "People will need to be told. We're not talking about some sort of dictatorship where you can ignore public opinion. I think you should let Mr Price have his interview. "

In fact, once Lomas had taken the plunge he turned out to be a good talker. They sat on opposite sides of the cabin table while the Admiral perched on the companionway steps nodding approval. It was obviously the first time he had heard much of the story. Price wrote furiously, hoping his shorthand could withstand the motion of the yacht. Lomas stared into space and told his story as if it was something he had wanted to get off his chest for a long time.

He didn't stop until he had brought Price right up to date.

Sir Charles held up his hand: "It's one thing to talk about what's already happened," he said. "But the rest still comes under the heading of Official Secrets."

Price could see he wasn't going to get round that. He only had one question: "Whose idea was this? It must have seemed extraordinary at the beginning. Who suggested it - was it you, Sir Charles?"

The old man looked at him as if he was debating whether to tell a lie or say nothing. In the end he said: "Yes, it was my idea. I discussed it with other people but the original suggestion came from me."

And Price knew he was lying. There was nothing he could put a finger on - only that he'd heard people lie before and he knew he was hearing it again. But he didn't say anything. He didn't want to foul things up for Channon.

Dave Channon knew exactly the picture he wanted. He'd spent almost a week thinking about it. Now he had to persuade the Commander to provide it.

A picture of the little sailing boat and the nuclear submarine meeting in the middle of the empty ocean," he said. "I'll take it from the dinghy at dawn."

But this was going too far. The Commander was adamant, and he was probably right: "You're asking me to expose my submarine on the surface in full daylight. You know I can't do that. It's unthinkable"

Channon opened his mouth to persuade him - and in his time, Channon had persuaded just about everyone from gangsters to royalty to pose for his camera.

But then the Admiral broke in once more. Still Price couldn't entirely understand why. But the old man said simply: "Maybe it's not such a risk." He gave his son an odd sort of look. Price wanted to ask why it shouldn't be such a risk. But suddenly they had an agreement and the moment was lost.

Channon immediately started issuing instructions. He wanted the submarine to surface to the west of the dinghy, so the sun would be behind the camera and he wanted the two vessels facing each other so it would look as though they were meeting in the middle of nowhere. He wanted the white ensign flying and the submarine moving slowly so he could get plenty of pictures.

And when all that was settled, he took them all down to the cabin to be photographed there and then. By the time Lomas pulled a walkie-talkie out of his pocket and called up his inflatable, he was as enthusiastic about the story as the newsmen. He shook Price by the hand and allowed himself to be put through the traditional promise that he would not talk to any other newspapers, radio or television stations and would contact Price as soon as he got back. Susan kissed him and clung to his arm for a moment. Then the Admiral shook him by the hand and said cryptically: "You'll be all right now, my boy." Lomas said: "Yes, I rather think we will." Then he swung his leg over the guardrails and climbed down into the inflatable and gave a last wave to the four of them clustered in the dark of the cockpit. After that the outboard started and he was gone.

*

Susan rowed Dave Channon out in the dinghy for his photo session. She sat paddling gently with the oars to give him a clear view of the yacht and the submarine together. He was working with two cameras, continually changing the lenses between them, altering the exposure as the sun went behind clouds and re-appeared again.

She had come to look on the newspapermen as a couple of friends and the unpleasantness at the beginning seemed a very long time ago. Yet now she had the feeling they were friendly and polite because it was what they needed to be to get their story and their pictures. If they thought they would succeed by being ruthless and bullying, then she had no doubt they would be just that.

She remembered the time she rang up Bernie in the middle of the night and tried to make a bargain with him. He simply refused, and she told him everything anyway. And now he had calmly taken over again and made Peter talk to him - and Dave Channon had Vanguard swanning about on the surface in broad daylight. They seemed to assume people would do what they wanted - and sure enough, people did. She found it uncanny and she didn't like it. It must, she decided, take a peculiar type of person to make a newspaperman.

Channon took some shots of Vanguard diving for the last time and then some more of Clarinda alone. Finally he looked up, flashed a big smile and said: "That's it, darlin'. Home we go. "

She spun the dinghy expertly on the top of a wave and headed back to the yacht. Channon lay in the stern singing "Row, row, row your boat, gently down the stream..."

She watched him and kept rowing.

SIXTEEN

Cosmos 2318 was 150 miles over the Stanovoi Mountains of Eastern Siberia when a burst of compressed air ejected the film canister.

An ageing Antonov 12 transport aircraft from the Soviet Air Force base at Gizhiga was already in the target zone. Its radio operator picked up the homing beacon even before the small orange parachute deployed at 8,000 metres. Within three minutes the pilot had visual contact and gave the order to stream the trapeze.

Two twenty metre cables, joined at intervals by cross wires and weighted at the ends, began to trail out of the tailgate until the whole contraption hung below and behind the aircraft like a gigantic rope ladder.

The pilot pulled the plane round in a banking turn until the little parachute, bright in the sunshine of the upper air, was in the centre of his windscreen and about two kilometres away. Then, with the ease that comes from long practise, he flew the Antonov above it until the parachute became a flash of orange disappearing under the nose.

In the cargo bay the loadmaster saw the scrap of material smack against one of the crosswires and instantly begin to flap itself to pieces in the slipstream. The pilot turned for home. Three sorties a day flying satellite recovery missions was nothing more than a mindless routine.

At Gizhiga the canister went straight to the aerial reconnaissance laboratory and the film was developed within the hour. A young Air Force officer examined the strip under a magnifying glass. As usual, frame after frame showed nothing but empty ocean. The sections showing land masses would be enlarged and analysed separately, so he ignored those too. But the few that showed shipping he marked for enlargement immediately.

By the time he reached the last of them the first few were being returned to him as large, floppy photographs still slightly damp. The merchantmen he dismissed, warships he put to one side. He would have to identify them all and telex their movements to Leningrad. Submarines were different, though. The new standing orders said that photographs of submarines should be wired immediately,

It was barely an hour after the last of them had gone that he received a phone call telling him to send one of the negatives. He was to have it flown to Leningrad by MIG 30Y. The Air Force officer was impressed. Anything that had to be flown from one side of the Soviet Union to the other at Mach 3 had to be very important indeed. He went back to the wire room and looked at the print. It showed a small pleasure boat and a submarine - a British Trident class submarine.

*

There was an urgency about the words "Captain to the control room" which silenced Vanguard's wardroom. They were past Ireland now and in deep water again but they still felt vulnerable. Lomas left his meal and went without a word. As he closed the sliding door behind him, he could hear the conversation start up again. Somebody said: "Must be a submarine contact."

If it was, then the chances were that it was Russian. The way the Soviets had been building them over the past twenty years, you could hardly move in the Atlantic without running into one. Normally Vanguard would go quiet and slip away. The Russians had never once tracked a British Trident submarine. It was different for the fleet boats. They could afford to play a good-natured sort of hide and seek.

This time Vanguard would be playing it too. This time she had to be found. Only when the Russian had analysed her sound signature and identified her could Lomas break off and disappear. It would be like playing chess and giving away half the pieces.

As he came into the control room, sonar reported: "Passive contact bearing 340 distant. He's definitely a submarine sir. Analysing now. "

Lomas stood for'ard of the periscope and waited. There was a faint blip on the outer edge of the display. Then finally: "Control: sonar. Contact is an Alpha bearing 340. Range 39 miles and closing." Quietly and firmly Lomas said: "Action stations. I have the boat."

The officer of the watch already had the microphone in his hand. The order sounded through the submarine. Men began moving to their stations, closing the watertight doors behind them.

Lomas checked the plot and started planning. A submarine hides in many ways. It hides from aircraft and satellites by diving. It hides from anti-submarine units by using the contours of the ocean floor and the different temperature layers in the water - the inversion layers. When the enemy is another submarine and the ocean bed is two miles beneath the keel, there is only one option. Lomas studied the temperature graph.

Inversion layers are unpredictable - more common in summer and mostly in the tropics. In the North Atlantic, he'd be lucky to find one when he wanted it. There was no good news in being up against an Alpha either. It was faster than Vanguard and with its titanium alloy hull, it could dive deeper - down to 1,500 metres, so the book said. He wouldn't be able to run. He wouldn't be able to bottom out. He was going to have to be crafty.

He plucked the microphone and punched the button for the pipe: "This is the Captain. We've just met one of our Russian friends - an Alpha. We're going to stick around just long enough to write our signature on his sonar screen and then I'd like to vanish." He paused. "The management apologise for any inconvenience."

One of the plotters, marking his screen with a chinagraph pencil, turned and grinned. Lomas smiled back, and Vanguard kept going - deep into the enemy's sonar range.

Then from the sound room: "Contact turning right. Track 270 and slowing." The Russian was turning for an intercept and reducing speed to try and stay hidden.

When the range had closed to 20 miles, Lomas began to ease gradually down. The trace on the temperature graph dropped steadily and then began to rise when they reached l50 metres. There was an inversion layer after all. Things were looking up. Lomas said: "Half power state. Revolutions for ten knots" and then: "Ten down. Port l5. Come to 225." The deck canted and Vanguard dropped sharply into the warmer water, effectively drawing a blanket of sound between herself and the Russian. After a minute or two sonar reported the contact lost. It was just possible the Russian could still hear them - sometimes sound travels through water in one direction better than another. But Lomas had little doubt the Alpha was on its way down.

Escape now depended on his next move. Evans was watching him, ready to anticipate the order. He could double back up but then he'd be followed once more and that could go on indefinitely. The time to get away was now, while the two submarines were still well separated. If he gave the impression of returning to the layer and then suddenly went quiet and dropped deep, the Russian would lose time searching for him above it. He levelled and straightened at 350 metres heading south west. Then he turned to Evans, but he spoke so that everyone in the control room could hear him: "We're going to make a break when the Alpha regains contact. I'll want to crack on 42 knots and go up l5. And while we're making all that racket

I want to trim for 700 metres."

Evans nodded solemnly, refusing to be surprised. Trimming for 700 meant giving the boat greater buoyancy - since at that depth the hull would be squeezed and effectively heavier. But dumping that much ballast at only l50 metres could send them out of control to the surface. Lomas went on: "Once the Alpha's lost us a second time, we stop everything, go quiet and with 42 knots momentum, we plane down, understood."

With some effort Evans said: "Aye aye, sir - and warned the manoeuvring room to expect a burst at full revs.

Then they waited. Vanguard crept along to the south west, giving every impression of a submarine trying to slink away. When the Russian captain picked up their sound again he'd think himself pretty clever.

Whatever the Russian captain was thinking, he wasn't being cautious. He came belting down at 30 knots plus. Sonar resumed the contact at a range of only l2 miles.

Lomas snapped out his orders: "Full power state. Revs for 42 knots. Up l5." He nodded to Evans and as the high-pressure air wailed through the pipes to the trimming tanks, Vanguard surged upwards, the growing buoyancy adding to her speed. Lomas watched the temperature graph intently. He'd have to guess this. At high speed and with the enemy behind him, the sonar watch was all but useless.

Then at l00 metres: "What's the speed?"

"Thirty-six knots, sir."

"O.K. for trim, Number One?"

"Trimmed for 700, sir."

"Right, all stop. Down l5, port ten. Come to l60."

Vanguard slewed round and down, her massive bulk taking over propulsion from her engine. Sonar reported a weak contact which must have been the Russian lunging upwards.

At 6l0 metres they coasted to a stop. Hovering in their element, silent and motionless.

They waited there for half an hour and then sonar reported the Russian hunting above and behind them, cruising back and forth like a blind man who put something down not a moment ago and suddenly can't find it. Occasionally he stopped to listen but the only sound Vanguard made in her quiet state was the faint hum of the reactor's pumps – and with the plant well damped down, that would not be enough.

Lomas imagined the Russian captain ruefully admitting defeat, standing his crew down and reverting to patrol routine. This was the end of the game. Now they would go their separate ways.

According to the rules of the game, it was for the Russian to make the first move. He should speed up, which in the clear sound signature to Vanguard's sonar room, was as good as saying; "O.K. you win" and then steam off on a steady course leaving Vanguard to get under way in her own time.

But the Russian didn't do that. He hunted around for

another six hours. This was all rather pointless. The watch changed. Lomas ate sandwiches in the control room - and all the while the Russian cruised slowly about above them, sometimes ten or fifteen miles away, sometimes only five. He had obviously worked out what Lomas had done - but that didn't help him pinpoint Vanguard now.

Then someone allowed a watertight door to slam. The noise reverberated through the boat. Evans screwed up his face in frustration. They waited, tense now. A one-off noise like that might be missed - but if it hadn't been - if the Russian now had something concrete to work on, they would have to go through the whole business again.

Then they all heard it together - the harsh clang against the hull. The sound room reported instantly: "Active sonar bearing 180 six thousand metres." The astonishment was evident in the operator's voice and for an instant Lomas was transfixed. Nobody used active sonar in these conditions. It instantly gave you away. The only possible reason for it was a final plotting for torpedo attack. It just didn't make sense. But Lomas didn't think about what made sense. He acted exactly as he'd been trained to. His next order was automatic: "Full power state, revolutions for maximum speed, ten down.

As Vanguard shivered with the effort of accelerating from a standing start, he added; "Stream a decoy." He was going to extraordinary lengths - but something was very wrong here.

Sonar cut in: "Torpedo discharged bearing 175 range

5,500."

Christ, it was for real. Starboard 15. What's the speed?"
"20 knots."

The Russian torpedoes could do almost seventy. Lomas' only hope lay in the decoy, even now dropping further and further astern on the end of its cable.

The speed built up, 25 knots ... 30 ... 40. Every minute cut down the rate the torpedo was gaining on them - and there was still no sign of the Russian firing a second. There had been a time when British Submarines fired their homing torpedoes singly to cut down the interference. The technicians at Faslane had got round it now - but the Soviets hadn't. With luck he could neutralise the entire attack. The critical thing was to judge the right moment to switch on the decoy - too soon and the Russian torpedo officer would not have cut the wires and could still order his weapon to ignore it - too late and the torpedo would have already overtaken the decoy.

Lomas studied the command display. He heard the reports coming in, he noted the orders of his officers - but all the time his concentration stayed fixed on the gradually merging points of light on the screen.

With 150 metres between the torpedo and the decoy, he said: "Activate the decoy." Then: "Starboard ten."

As Vanguard swung away from the path of the torpedo, its image on the screen appeared to move left, the homing system was locked on the decoy.

They heard the explosion before sonar reported it.

Immediately he swung in a tight banking turn that had the control room team bracing themselves against their equipment. Now it was they who were on the attack.

"Stand by for Tigerfish attack. Two torpedoes. Stream a decoy."

The two submarines were now racing towards each other with a closing speed of more than seventy knots - but there was no alternative. There was hardly time for the torpedo course calculator to reach a solution before sonar came on with "Firing bearing cut."

Then Lomas, who had never fired a torpedo in anger in his life, said: "Fire."

The reports came in a flurry:

"Both torpedoes running."

"Torpedo discharged bearing 205 range 3,000." That was the Russian firing again. He'd left it too late. Lomas had the advantage. Not only did he have two torpedoes running but he'd fired sooner. That meant he could turn away sooner.

It all happened very quickly then. He cut the wires leaving the Tigerfish 500 metres to run and turned, banking sharply. The enemy torpedo had 1,000 metres to go and now had to overhaul him.

"Target drawing right."

The Russian was turning away, trying the same trick. Now he too would have to chop the wires. The three torpedoes threshing in opposite directions were on their own.

Lomas watched the display with morbid fascination, his own torpedoes diminishing in intensity, the enemy's growing brighter.

Then he heard the explosion. He could hear it still rumbling through the water even as sonar reported the Russian decoy destroyed. But there was still the enemy's fish on his tail. He threw Vanguard around the ocean, swooping up, turning and banking, drawing the decoy time and again across its nose.

Somewhere in the middle of everything else, he heard: "Explosion on target bearing." That could only be a hit - but it would mean nothing if Vanguard herself were sunk. Sonar carried on with routine reports of implosion sounds on the target bearing but no-one gave any sign of being distracted. The Russian's last torpedo was closing fast, bent on revenge.

Lomas watched it on the display: "Starboard ten, six down, 300 metres." And the spark on the screen began to veer away to the left, closing with the decoy.

When the explosion came it was close, very close. It picked up Vanguard and flung the submarine bodily forwards and upwards. Lomas grabbed at the periscope to save himself from falling. Pencils and clipboards, cups and half the loose paraphernalia of the control room cascaded to the deck.

And then everything went quiet. Lomas ordered all stop for a sonar sweep. Even without it he could hear the distorted rending sounds of the Russian submarine being crushed as it dropped into the increasing pressure of deep water. There would be men inside it still alive. fighting against the ocean that poured in on them - and there wasn't one in Vanguard's control room who didn't realise that it could so easily have been the other way round.

They didn't cheer. They didn't clap each other on the back. Nobody spoke. They sat, facing to the front, staring at their consoles. Lomas felt proud of them for that.

There would be those in the after-ends who had only the sketchiest idea of what had happened. He didn't feel like saying anything. He felt drained and confused, but he took up the microphone, paused for a second and then pressed the button: "This is the Captain. We have torpedoed and sunk a Soviet Alpha which attacked us with torpedoes. I don't know why any more than you do - it's something we can only hope will become clear in time.

"Meanwhile despite whatever anxieties we must all feel at this moment, I want to say thank you for the way you've all worked in the past few hours. We trained hard for this and it paid off. Well done."

Evans was watching him, he thought with an expression of sympathy. Lomas said: "Thank you, Number One. Stand down now."

SEVENTEEN

It was Private Eye which first brought the whole thing out into the open.

Vincent Earlham was not surprised. There had even been a time when he had approved of the little magazine's determination to uncover a scandal - any scandal - with or without the facts to back it up.

It should have been obvious the Eye could never be fobbed off with excuses about not enough space at the dockyard for all the submarines - and even Earlham himself was getting fed up with the Ministry's constant whine that it "never discussed movements of nuclear submarines".

Private Eye didn't need any help from the Ministry, its "l00 Years Ago" column managed to get uncomfortably close to the truth with just the occasional fact and a lot of innuendo:

The Peace Movement's eagerly awaited Trident-scrapping beano seems no nearer.

Despite MOD refusals to discuss anything at all, word comes from the Vickers dockyard at Barrow that when the fourth covered dry dock became vacant last week with the launching of the new minesweeper HMS Lymington, its place was immediately taken by the ageing destroyer HMS Brazen and not the mysteriously missing sub HMS Vanguard after all.

Meanwhile the team of technicians called in to dismantle the reactors of the other three submarines are delighted to find they're to go on leave before tackling the fourth monster.

Asked why the salvation of the human race should be delayed for the hols, the newly converted Peace People of Whitehall confessed to "no knowledge" of such a development which seems strange since they were the ones who drafted the order.

Earlham knew that it wouldn't be long before he'd have to answer a question in Parliament and he wasn't going to tell a lie.

At least, that's what he told the Prime Minister.

Tattersall looked tired - not just overworked but weary with the whole business; almost bored.

He said: "If you're so determined to tell the truth, perhaps you'd better read it first." He took a red folder from his drawer and dropped it on the front of the desk.

The folder stayed there for a long moment as Earlham looked carefully at the Prime Minister and Tattersall sat slouched in this chair like an arrogant schoolboy. Earlham was beginning to get a very bad feeling about this. He picked up the folder and started to read.

From time to time he looked up and stared at Tattersall. He couldn't believe the man could have been so stupid. He had behaved like a dictator - he even had this Carling man running his personal secret police.

Earlham said: "We won't survive it, you know. This is going to come out and when it does we're finished."

Tattersall sat there almost as if he didn't care.

"You've thrown it all away, you know. We were almost there. We practically achieved something which people have been striving for since the early 50's. And now we've betrayed them - *you've* betrayed them."

Tattersall seemed to shrug. Earlham got up and began to pace about. It made him feel less helpless. He went on: "I warned you but you wouldn't listen. I told you that if we'd made a clean breast of it straight away, announced that a renegade naval officer had run off with a Trident submarine, the sympathy would have been all on our side. Our case against an irresponsible military would be been proven. Now who's irresponsible?

"What on earth possessed you to use this detective in the first place? And as for this attempt to ambush a submarine; why, it's laughable."

Tattersall looked up sharply, as if at last he was showing some interest. He snapped: "They'd been tipped off. They turned back before they reached the beach. He couldn't have foreseen that."

Earlham looked at his Prime Minister and said nothing for the moment. He wondered if Tattersall was becoming paranoid. He had handled it badly throughout. He had relied on amateurish tricks and he had abused his power.

And now he was whining on: "It doesn't make any difference anyway. Limpkin says they'd never launch these missiles without orders and they can't get them now the computer program's been destroyed."

Earlham stared at him. The man really believed it. Very patiently he explained: "You're losing sight of the real issue. How much do you think the Soviets will trust us once they know we've deceived our own people? Who'd expect them to disarm in Eastern Europe after this - and think of the effect on the movement in the America. Since we came to power, they've begun to realise that they can change the system. What do you suppose will happen when they discover they've been conned and in fact the answer's: 'No, nothing can be changed - nuclear disarmament is impossible.' They'll turn away in droves."

Earlham sat down then. There was a long and heavy silence and the Prime Minister looked at his desk and bit his lip. If he knew what he had to do, he was too proud to say it. Earlham gave him his answer anyway: "We've got to stop being so damned secretive about it. We need more people involved. We need more opinion. You can do what you like but I'm going to talk to the under secretaries and the disarmament policy committee."

He waited for Tattersall to say something - to argue with him or agree with him. But he said nothing. He just sat there, staring into space. Earlham picked up the file and left without waiting to be shown out. As he emerged into the outer office, a private secretary leapt to his feet but Vincent Earlham ignored him and went on down to his car.

If he was honest with himself, he could see no way out of the mess at all. But he had the best tactical brains in the world peace community on his side and he was going to use them. As he walked into his office, the Permanent Secretary fell into step beside him. Before he reached his desk, he was issuing instructions to set up the committee.

Before he sat down he pulled the red folder out of his briefcase and said: "I want a copy of this for every member."

And as he started to write, he could already hear the permanent secretary calling: "Miss Crichton, we'll need fourteen copies of this."

*

SYNOPSIS

Meeting of the Politburo of the Central Committee of the Communist Party of the Soviet Union. August 16th 1999. Item 1 (special projects).

Comrade the Supreme Commander Naval Forces presented his report on the attempted destruction of the British Trident class submarine Vanguard (Appendix A). He advised the committee that it must now be presumed that the Soviet vessel was destroyed in the engagement. He further advised the committee that it was not certain the British submarine had been destroyed. Units of the Soviet Navy were searching the area. Comrade the chairman observed that if the British submarine had survived the engagement, its crew would now be doubly cautious and it must be doubtful that any trace would be found.

Members criticised Comrade the Supreme Commander Naval Forces for his handling of the operation. There was discussion regarding the effect of this uncertainty on plans for the intended conventional strike into Western Europe.

Comrade the Marshall of the Red Army advised the committee that it was essential that all western nuclear weapons should be destroyed before any campaign was launched. He warned that any other course might well lead to unacceptably high losses.

Comrade the Director of Security Services reported the results of covert operations in London which provided new information about the British submarine Vanguard and also about attempts by the British Government to force its return to port (Appendix B).

The Director of Security Services presented a report from the KGB technical services branch (Appendix C) suggesting that the remote controlled explosive device fitted to the submarine by the British security service might now be used to assist the Soviet Navy. Advice from the technical services branch suggested that a detonating device similar to the one employed by the British but of considerably greater power could be used to cause an explosion from a range of many kilometres.

Comrade the Supreme Commander Naval Forces welcomed the proposal and advised members that such an explosion, even if it failed to destroy the submarine, would certainly assist units of the Soviet Navy in locating it and bringing about its assured destruction.

Resolutions: The resolutions were carried unanimously that:

i) The Security Service should obtain the British device or, failing that, details of its construction and the frequencies needed to trigger an explosion.
ii) That similar detonating devices with increased power should be prepared and installed aboard units of the Soviet Navy.
iii) That plans for a conventional strike into Western Europe should be postponed pending more information on Britain's nuclear capability.

*

Elizabeth was happy. She was allowed to talk to Lorenz every evening. Never for more than a few minutes, of course, but it was enough just to hear his voice and to know that he was alive. They were making plans now, plans for the day they would be together again. They were going away to Greece or North Africa - anywhere there would still be some summer left.

She had convinced herself that it wouldn't be long now. With every piece of information she passed, ever document she laboriously typed into the little machine, she could feel herself coming closer and closer to Lorenz.

She no longer thought that what she was doing was wrong. It never occurred to her any more that she was a spy. Instead she saw herself as a sort of nurse - the harder she worked, the better Lorenz would get until one day she could bring him home.

Her social life had virtually ceased to exist. She had given up her dance classes but sat at home late into the night typing, endlessly typing - and when she did get to bed, she had to wake again only an hour or two later to transmit the documents.

That was probably why she dreamed so much. Mostly she dreamed of Lorenz. She dreamed of their picnics in the mountains and she saw vague images of their life together when all this would be over. Sometimes the dreams were overtly sexual, and she woke suddenly, confused but exhilarated - and the dreams spilled over into her days so that she was aware of people giving her curious glances and had to force herself to concentrate.

But at the weekends she indulged herself. She took to walking aimlessly around London for hours at a time until she suddenly came to her senses miles from home. Then, exhausted, she would get a taxi back to her flat and fall straight into bed and sleep the night through.

On the Sunday when everything finally became clear, she had set out with the vague idea of buying a pair of bright yellow jeans. She walked down Notting Hill, looking in the windows, occasionally going into stores to sort idly through the clothes on the racks. But gradually she became less interested in looking than she was in walking. She turned into Kensington Church Street and walked steadily south, seeing only the people but never their faces. She crossed Kensington High Street and went on down into Earls Court. She thought constantly about Lorenz. If he had been with her she would have bought the jeans. She imagined them walking hand in hand. Even that was special with him because of his finger. She smiled to herself as she realised she even loved his imperfection. She loved him so very much.

When she saw him through the window of the restaurant, she stood staring at him foolishly, thinking how boyish he looked with his short hair. In a moment he would look up and be surprised to see her. Then he would smile that lovely, lop-sided smile of his and get up, correct as ever. But it wasn't surprise that made him interrupt the man sitting opposite. It was fright.

She blinked uncertainly and gradually the rest of the scene came into focus. The other man, staring at her over his menu, was Zimmermann - that couldn't be right. And there too was the other one, the one with the close-cropped hair she had last seen wearing a T-shirt, hitting Lorenz with his huge ugly hands and keeping him strapped in that chair with that awful thing...

Yet now they were all having lunch together as if they were friends. She felt herself swaying as she tried to take it in, tried to make sense of what she was seeing, to link it somehow with images which had taken root in her mind over the past weeks. She saw flashes of what was going on in front of her as if she was watching a disjointed film. The three men talking urgently to each other, Lorenz getting up and then sitting down again, looking up at her quickly and then back to Zimmermann. She saw him push back his spindly little chair so that it fell against the woman sitting behind him. She watched him struggling through the close-packed tables, looking anxiously back at her so that he brushed past the other customers and a red-shirted waiter had to hurry out of his path. Then, at the door he had to wait while a couple went in and she saw him looking between them, staring at her with an expression she had never seen before. His face was grim and cruel and something inside her brain clicked into place. She knew she had to get away.

She ran. At first, she ran sobbing and stumbling, knowing that he was just behind her, expecting to feel his hand on her shoulder, spinning her round. She could hear his footsteps and then a commotion as he collided with a passer-by. But when he didn't catch her in the first 20 metres, her head cleared and she shook the tears out of her eyes. She tucked her thumb into the strap of her shoulder bag, pulled up her head and ran like the wind.

There were people all over the pavement, couples hand in hand, mothers with prams and push chairs. People who stopped and stared as she dodged and weaved around them so that behind her. Lorenz found his way blocked by a succession of immovable backs.

The speed was exhilarating. It gave her some sort of release and that made her run faster still. She was outrunning him. She didn't feel tired or breathless, even though she could tell from the shouting behind her that Lorenz was flagging.

Now the initiative was hers. She would double back on herself, confuse him - leave him standing uncertainly in the middle of the pavement, staring about him and wondering which way to go. She looked quickly into side streets as she came to them, but none had turnings leading off. One was a cul-de-sac which would have been terrible.

Then she saw a bus - a beautiful red London bus. It stood waiting at the stop 50 metres away as the last of the queue filed aboard. She sprinted the distance and slipped through the doors just as they closed. She stuffed a handful if coins into the machine and went through the turnstile, pausing only when the driver put the bus into gear and began to edge forward. But then it stopped, there was a truck parked in front of them and the driver had to wait for a gap in the traffic.

She stood there, holding onto the handrail and willing the bus to move. Lorenz appeared outside. He was red in the face and breathing hard. He put his hands up against the Perspex of the door, appealing to the driver. But the driver knew the rules. He pressed down once more on the accelerator and the bus shuddered and began to move.

Suddenly Elizabeth felt unsteady. She closed her eyes and then shook her head to clear it. She fumbled her way to a seat by the window and looked back. Lorenz was still on the pavement, staring into the traffic, waving at a taxi which was already full and drove past him, overtaking the bus.

Elizabeth closed her eyes and her head fell forward. An old woman sitting behind her tapped her on the shoulder and said anxiously: "You all right, love?"

Elizabeth nodded, unable to speak.

*

The whole thing had been a disaster from the start. Lorenz stood at the roadside, breathing hard and blaming other people. What kind of idiot picked a restaurant as a dead letter box? What was wrong with leaving envelopes inside the cisterns of public lavatories or in newspapers left on park benches - or the hollow trunk of a tree for God's sake? What possessed the lunatics to tape it to the underside of a restaurant table? He turned and walked back. It had been his fault as much as anyone's. He had been the one who wanted to tag along. One meal, he had said, wouldn't do any harm. The chances of running into one girl in the whole of London were infinitesimal.

But now she knew everything. He wondered whether he could salvage anything at all. He could threaten to expose her but her kind usually didn't care what happened to them once they reached this stage. He could offer to take her back to Moscow, play the love scene once more - but she wouldn't fall for it a second time; he knew her well enough to be sure of that. No, if the operation was to continue, they would have to find some other source. She would have to be eliminated. He would prefer not to have to do it himself. He walked slowly back towards the restaurant. The car, cruising aimlessly in the hope of catching up with the chase. pulled up beside him. Gregor moved to the back seat and he climbed in beside Zimmermann.

The older man looked at him: "Well?"

"I lost her. She got on a bus." Zimmermann knew better than to criticise him.

"She'll be no good now. Better she's out of the way. Gregor can do it. A suicide would be best. she's the type - single woman living alone. Make it pills."

They drove to the girl's flat and dropped Gregor around the corner. They watched him walk off - a big man with very short hair, that's all anyone ever remembered about Gregor.

Zimmermann pulled the car round and took a brown envelope from his inside pocket. The adhesive tape which had held it to the restaurant table was now bunched around it in a sticky mess. Lorenz took it and ripped it open. Inside was £500 in old notes. There was also a tape cassette. It featured a pop group Lorenz had vaguely heard of. He pulled out a length of tape and looked at the back, shifting it along between his fingers until he came to the cyrillic type. He read in silence for a minute or two.

Beside him Zimmermann kept driving towards

Hammersmith. After a while he said: "What now?"

"Find the device which detonates the mine on the submarine."

Zimmermann snorted: "It can't be far. This is a fairly small island."

Lorenz smiled. "No, it can't be far. Perhaps we should ask a policeman..."

EIGHTEEN

The Ministry of Defence duty intelligence officer was on call. That meant he lay in a heavy brocade armchair in the living room of his rather old fashioned suburban home. His wife was clearing away remains of Sunday lunch but the intelligence officer was fast asleep and snoring softly. He did not wake when the telephone rang, and he became cross and confused when his wife shook him.

It was not the sort of matter that should have been referred to him anyway. The weekend staff at Whitehall should have had more sense. If a girl at the Ministry got herself into some kind of scrape, then she should tell her superiors. They were the ones who knew her - they could decide whether all this talk of spies was anything more than just a schoolgirl fancy. Only then, as he explained at some length, should the intelligence branch be called in.

But it seemed the girl was distraught, and the weekend staff felt this was a matter of urgency and basically - it was becoming very obvious they felt sorry for her. That was presumably easy enough if you hadn't just enjoyed a good lunch and most of a bottle of claret.

The duty intelligence officer sent his wife upstairs for a jacket, climbed into his two-year-old Vauxhall and set out for some hotel he had never heard of in North Kensington with all the enthusiasm of a man who has reached middle age, the rank of Major and the realisation that he will never go any further. Porky Johnson was just going through the motions.

*

Elizabeth had washed her face with the harsh hotel soap, but her eyes were still red-rimmed from crying. Make-up did a lot to hide her blotched and puffy skin but in the end it was the eyes that gave her away.

She looked hard into the mirror above the washbasin. The silvering had worn away with age and she had to stand to one side to frame her face between the black patches on the glass. She looked at herself and said aloud: "O.K?"

She'd be all right now. She'd been through this before. A man used you and cheated you and you went off to live alone and said you didn't need anyone - until, of course, you found you did.

It was odd, really, that she could spend so much time thinking about that side of things when she knew quite well she had very nearly been killed. She'd known that at once. One look at Lorenz's face as he came at her through the restaurant door had told her that - yet somehow the idea of him as murderer and herself as victim was unimportant now. It was all finished. Nothing, it seemed, would really matter again. She would be sent to prison, she supposed. Not for long, maybe, once they heard what had happened - and she was definitely doing the right thing, giving herself up.

But her eyes still looked haunted.

*

"For the past four months I have regularly supplied secret information to a Soviet agent."

Major Johnson heard the words and stared at the girl perched on the worn bedspread and wondered whether to believe her. It didn't sound like the ramblings of some silly filing clerk. This was an intelligent young woman who had reached a difficult decision and now she was desperately holding onto her emotions while she went through with what she had decided to do.

One way and another it was a job for MI6, for people who knew about spies and interrogations and that sort of thing. Major Johnson realised he was out of his depth. But at the same time, he had the feeling that if this girl didn't get it off her chest soon, she'd lose her nerve and then no-one would be able to get it out of her and besides, he couldn't very well call in MI6 without knowing quite what he was letting them in for. He made a passable effort at sounding sympathetic and said: "Would you like to tell me about it?"

It was a classic tale, of course. The East Germans had perfected the technique in Belgium with the NATO secretaries, although this was obviously much more sophisticated. He even felt a certain amount of sympathy for the girl - what would he have done in her place? As she relaxed and told her story, he was rather surprised to find himself taking something of a professional interest. He even pulled out his diary and noted down the odd fact on the blank pages at the back. There were various steps which ought to be taken straight away: The restaurant would have to be checked and there might also have been a car. The girl's home would need to be watched in case they tried to contact her again.

He wondered if she could be used as bait - probably not. Any agent capable of setting up this sort of operation would realise he was blown and make a clean break. The other side wouldn't give up, of course. They'd be back, looking for another way to get at the same information...

He stopped her then and said: "What kind of stuff did they want? Was it just any secret document or something in particular?"

She blinked at him. He thought she was going to ask him what difference it made. But she explained very patiently: "Nuclear disarmament. They wanted anything at all to do with nuclear disarmament. I sent lists of weapons and where they were stored, schedules for transporting them - all sorts of things. They were very keen on seeing anything that was going to Number Ten. There was a lot of stuff marked for the P.M. personally - mostly about HMS Vanguard."

"What about HMS Vanguard?"

"Well, about it not being scrapped. About the crew taking it off on their own."

Major Johnson stared at her. She stopped then. Almost

apologetically, she said: "Didn't you know?"

This girl knew the answers to questions the rest of the country had been asking for weeks. While rumours had been running through all three armed services and most of the Ministry of Defence as well, this slip of a girl knew the truth. She knew it and she had been too wrapped up in her ruddy boyfriend to realise what it meant.

Very gently he got her to tell him everything she knew.

What he heard appalled him. There would be the mother and father of a row over this. There would have to be an inquiry, of course. But if that happened, the first thing to come out would be the role of the Government - and most important, the part the Prime Minister had played. No. they'd never hold an inquiry. Yet the Soviets were interested enough to mount a sophisticated operation to find out what was going on which, incidentally, had only failed through the most unlikely piece of luck. He sat there with the girl looking at him and thought about what would happen if he did what he was supposed to do and passed it on to MI6. It was entirely possible they would deal with her under the Official Secrets Act. She would be tried for spying, there would be the usual security scare but what she had given to the Moscow would remain secret in the national interest. To put it another way, it would not be in the "National Interest" for anyone to know that the British Prime Minister had tried to sabotage a British submarine.

Major Johnson found himself sweating. For the first time in a 32-year military career he began to make a really important decision. He was vaguely aware that he might be getting himself into very big trouble indeed, but he knew exactly where the Army stood on the idea of unilateral nuclear disarmament and he knew the best way to stop anything being hushed up was to get it right out in the open good and early. He told the girl to stay in the room and went down to the public phone in the lobby and called Bernie Price.

The newspaperman sounded rushed and distracted. It seemed he had people ringing him all day saying they had something vital to tell him but couldn't say any more over the telephone.

Major Johnson took a worried look around and turned his face to the wall. He explained: "One of those Trident submarines really has disappeared. The Government knows all about it."

"Yes, I know - HMS Vanguard," said Price down the line.

The Major stopped: "What do you mean. you know?"

"Everyone suspects it. I happen to know. It's just that I can't write it."

"Oh, then you know about the Russians - this man Lorez Erhardt. You know about the bomb on the submarine?"

There was a pause from the other end. Then: "What?"

*

Price started making phone calls. He called Susan Lomas: "Can you get in touch with Sir Charles. I've got to see him at once."

For a moment he thought she was going to start asking questions but instead he could sense her forcing herself to be calm and efficient. She had a phone number. She didn't know who it was but they could pass on a message.

Next Price rang the paper's crime correspondent at home. The man's young son answered and for several moments there were the sounds of domestic chaos with people shouting up and down stairs and dogs barking before the crime man came on.

Price said: "Colin, have you ever heard of a policeman called Carling. He's Mike Tattersall's personal bodyguard."

There was a pause at the end of the line, then: "There used to be a Carling in anti-terrorist. That might be the one. What about him?"

"I want to know where he lives."

Dave Channon was not at home. But underneath his address in the picture desk contacts book were the numbers of three south London pubs. Price found him in the second one.

"The Vanguard thing's moving again. Now there's a bomb on it."

Channon promptly stopped moaning about his day off. Price left for the hotel then. He wanted to be able to do the explaining before the others arrived. He would have preferred not to get the Admiral involved at all but a bomb scare was a bomb scare whether it happened in a nuclear submarine or the local Woolworths and you couldn't very well keep it to yourself.

As soon as he arrived, he phoned the crime correspondent again but there was still no news on the policeman's address. A contact at Scotland Yard was finding it. Price read over the number of the payphone and went up to see this Crichton woman.

The first thing that struck him was that she was in some kind of a trance. He shook a small limp hand and tried to look into a pair of grey eyes which didn't seem to notice him at all. She sat there quietly while Porky Johnson ran through the story again.

But it was the girl's version which counted. Price tried to draw her into the conversation but mostly he got "yes" and "no". He sent the Major out for three miniatures of Haig from the slot machine on the landing.

The whisky brought a little colour to her cheeks and gradually she became more animated. She talked awkwardly of the brief affair with the man Erhardt. He asked her straight out if she still loved him - it was best that way.

She looked puzzled and he wondered if she was going to refuse to answer, say it was none of his business. But then she said: "No, I don't think I do, not now. But perhaps that's because I don't think I can feel anything anymore. Perhaps otherwise I would. "

She was magic. He pulled out a notebook and helped her over the mock torture. She found that harder, but he needed it as much as the rest.

Dave Channon came in. He'd left his camera bag outside, but Price could see the telltale lump of a compact Nikon slung beneath his jacket. He waved the photographer into silence and the girl kept talking as if she hadn't noticed. Finally she said: "What's going to happen now, Mr Price?"

It startled Price that she should have turned to him rather than the Major. After all Porky was one of her own kind, a civil servant. Perhaps she was taken in by Price's professional concern, like someone at confession.

"They won't charge you," he said. "Not when they know there's all this to come out in a trial."

He tried to smile when he said it. But the truth was that once this got into print, there wouldn't be any surprises left. Rather gruffly, he decided it was time to introduce Channon. The photographer smiled his standard, winning smile. Price said: "Dave would like to take your picture. Just so we've got one, you understand."

Channon was still working when there was a knock at the door and the Admiral walked in. Price had forgotten all about him.

*

Elizabeth took one look at the white-haired old man standing stiffly in the doorway and felt her heart sink. She had been doing so well too. She hadn't cried when the Major came round and since Bernie Price arrived she had really pulled herself together. But now this fierce old man stood there and pointed at her and said: "Who's this?" as if she were some sort of exhibit.

Bernie was marvellous. He obviously felt embarrassed and maybe even a little angry. He took over completely and made a great show of introducing her, saying: "Miss Crichton knows probably more about what's happened to Vanguard than anyone else and she's agreed to help us."

That put the Admiral in his place and Elizabeth was astonished to find herself shaking his hand and saying: "Sir Charles, of course. I've read all about you..."

He looked startled, just a quizzical old man and she felt immeasurably better as she added: "...in Inspector Carling's reports..."

She thought she could detect a chuckle from Bernie Price and when the Admiral asked her about the bomb on the submarine, it was a request and not an order. All the same, there wasn't much she could tell him: "I only found out about it in the last file I sent to Zimmermann. That was the big one, the one with everything in it right from the beginning. It must have been fifty pages long. I remember it took me from the time I got home to the early hours of the morning to type it all into the machine.

"You've got to remember I was in rather an odd state of mind anyway. worrying about what they would do to Lorenz. By the time I finished typing my head was swimming. You can't expect me to remember everything. "

The Admiral started to say something about how vital it was they found this bomb, but Bernie put his hand on her arm and said: "Don't worry. It'll come back to you. Just tell us what you do remember. "

She smiled at him and started again: "I know Inspector Carling got a frogman to fix the bomb to the submarine. The idea was that if the captain didn't do as he was told and go straight to the dockyard, they could set it off by remote control. "No-one even knows if the frogman finished the job. They think he drowned. Believe me, it was just one small incident in the middle of a very long and detailed report which I was copy typing while thinking of something else entirely. You can't expect me to remember it all."

But they did. They waited patiently, and she tried her best. She imagined herself sitting once again at the table in her flat with the machine in front of her, the little green dot dancing across the screen dragging the words behind it. But when she tried to recall what the words were saying, she thought only of Lorenz. It made her shiver to realise the state she had got herself into over the man. Perhaps she was odd. Perhaps other people were more practical about these things and could keep their lives in perspective. It was a moment or two before she realised no-one was paying attention to her anyway. There was a young woman at the door saying Mr Price was wanted on the telephone. They sat in silence until he came back.

*

The crime correspondent was as good as his word: "It's going to cost you a large one, Bernie but I've got Carling's address."

Price breathed heartfelt thanks into the phone. No matter what Elizabeth Crichton might say. He knew he could never publish anything about London policemen putting bombs on British submarines without some kind of confirmation from the man himself. If this worked, he would have both ends of the story and no lawyer would run a pencil through it.

But once again, he'd forgotten about the Admiral. As soon as he got back into the room, brandishing the address in his notebook and saying, "Carling's in Wandsworth", Sir Charles held out his hand and said: "I'll take that."

Price stopped in his tracks. This couldn't be happening. "Listen, I got this. You wouldn't even know about it if it wasn't for me. You can come along if you like and you're welcome but you're not freezing us out at this stage."

The old man's eyes widened momentarily so that Price could see the whites all round the pupils. Sir Charles had been giving orders all his life and he was accustomed to having them obeyed. Price remembered how he had been in the Chairman's office, talking about the "highest authority" behind all this - authority so high he wouldn't even give it a name.

He said again; "I'll take that, Mr Price. This is not a matter for your newspaper. Men's lives are at stake here. You will remain behind."

This was too much for Dave Channon. He stepped up beside Price: "Now hang on a minute. We've got an agreement, remember. We're all in this together. Like the three musketeers - one for all and all for one - except we're sporting types and we're not going to use anything until it's O.K. by you. But you're not bloody leaving us behind."

Sir Charles looked from one to the other. Price wondered if he was considering trying to snatch the notebook. But instead he relaxed. He smiled unpleasantly and said in a voice quiet with overbearing logic: "Very well then, we shall stay here and if for any reason that bomb explodes before I am able to get a message to Vanguard, telling them where it's hidden and how to disarm it, I shall have no hesitation in explaining quite fully why I was delayed. I think your newspaper might be rather embarrassed: I don't imagine the public look too kindly on newspapers whose journalists behave irresponsibly in pursuit of their 'scoops'."

The old bastard: He was right of course. If it did come to the crunch nobody was going to be terribly impressed with the word of an ordinary reporter against a retired admiral and a knight of the garter to boot. Price tore the sheet out of his notebook and almost threw it at him.

"Thank you." Sir Charles now became businesslike again. He looked at Johnson: "You have some identification on you, Major? We may need that. Please come with me."

He was half way to the door when he stopped. Elizabeth Crichton was still sitting on the bed. It was quite obvious he had no further use for her but on the other hand, he clearly didn't want to leave her with Price and Channon. But it was the Major who said: "I think Miss Crichton should come with us, Sir. I am responsible for her safety." Price shot him a vitriolic glance - outranked, he supposed.

NINETEEN

They had once been workmen's houses. Now they had smart bay windows and the occasional sports car parked outside.

It didn't look like the sort of place you would expect a policeman to live but if the KGB London bureau said this was where to find Carling, then this was where Lorenz would look.

Right now, he was looking for a movement in the curtains. the glint of a binocular lens catching the light from a streetlamp.

Zimmermann drove at an even pace down the road. He was nervous as well. They were doing this too fast and they both knew it. If you wanted to take a man in his own home you should do it when he's asleep. But it was entirely possible that the girl hadn't gone home, that Gregor had not 'taken care' of her. If she'd raised the alarm then it was almost certain that behind the front door of Inspector Carling's little terraced house they would find a small army of Special Branch men.

Without a word Zimmermann drove round the corner and parked. He put the keys under the seat in case only one of them should make it back. Lorenz took a large battery-powered lantern from the parcel shelf and then they separated - Zimmermann making for Carling's street and Lorenz turning into the one running behind it.

He counted the houses to find the one that backed onto

the policeman's. It was no good. The lights were on and the gap between the curtains flickered with the light of a television set. The neighbouring houses were the same. In the end he picked one a few doors away. It was being renovated and there was builders' rubble in the garden but it still had the original front door with rotten wood and an old lock. Lorenz took a small run and tried to force it quietly. He succeeded only in bruising his shoulder. The second time he flung himself hard against the lock and felt the door spring open - the old wood splintered around it.

The hall was stacked with decorator's materials and almost at once he tripped over a large plastic bucket. He propped it against the broken door. Then with his hand over the lantern and just enough light to find his way, he went through to the kitchen. It was almost finished and looked exactly like a magazine advertisement for modern living. The back-door key was on one of the colour co-ordinated work surfaces. He let himself out.

The gardens were easier. There were coal bunkers and garbage bins to climb on and just enough light to see his way. He ended up in the garden directly behind Carling's. He pulled four panels out of the wooden fence and climbed through.

With a sense of overwhelming relief, he looked into the detective's brightly lit kitchen window. There were no curtains and he could see it was completely empty. Better yet. he could see through a wide serving hatch into the living room and there, sitting in an armchair and watching television was a well-built man of about 35. He looked exactly as anyone would expect an off-duty policeman to look.

Lorenz stepped back behind some sort of potting shed and shone the beam of the lantern up into the sky. The column of light showed up clearly for maybe twenty metres. For good measure he played it on the chimney of the next house where Zimmermann could not fail to see it. He flashed it on and off three times.

*

Carling was not used to boredom. Sure, he had spent mindless hours watching empty houses, whole nights sitting outside hotel rooms - but that was the job. That had never bored him. Now it was different. Now he knew he would be bored tomorrow too and there was nothing to be gained by it. His whole existence had suddenly become worthless. He was finished as a police officer. The Special Branch would never forgive him, and the Prime Minister would never protect him. His career was over, and he knew nothing else.

If he'd been a different type of man, he might have admitted he was depressed. He might have pulled himself together or just given up and got drunk. As it was he sat in front of the meaninglessly chattering television and felt sorry for himself.

When the doorbell rang, he went to answer it without

enthusiasm or curiosity. The man on the step was short and middle aged and said, "Mr Carling? May I come in, I have something urgent to discuss with you."

And Carling shrugged and let him in. He was past caring.

The stranger came into the living room and looked around as if he expected to find someone else there. Almost as if he was nervous. It seemed an odd sort of gesture, but who cared. He waved the man to a chair.

But the visitor didn't sit down. Instead he put his hand inside his jacket on the left side. He might have been reaching for his wallet. But a man who reaches for a wallet keeps his thumb forward to grasp it. A detective who spends his working days watching for assassins will notice things like that - and even in the dulled and embittered mind of Detective Inspector Donald Carling, a small alarm sounded. This was something he knew. This was something he had been trained in, trained to the point that he no longer had to think but acted on pure reflex.

As the man's hand emerged from his jacket holding a silenced automatic pistol, Carling was already swaying to his right. It simply never occurred to him to do anything else - just as it was a natural reaction for his left hand to snap out, forcing the gun to the wall. With his right, he applied an outside wrist lock, turning the barrel back at his attacker, just as he would in training.

The moves followed each other like the numbered paragraphs in the manual. As the pressure came on the wrist, the man's legs buckled... continuous pressure on the elbow joint... the fingers opened, and the gun fell to the floor. Carling put his foot on it.

The process went on - controlled, unhurried restraint and arrest. All he had to do was reach down and pick up the weapon...

Then suddenly everything went wrong. An almighty crash of glass from the kitchen and there was another man in the room. But this one was younger and faster and didn't make mistakes. He came through the door at the run, shards of glass falling from his hair and clothes. He landed feet apart and crouching - his own silenced automatic pointing directly at Carling's chest.

After the one brief explosion of sound, it was quiet enough to hear the murmur of breathing. Then, very gently, with a kind of exaggerated patience, the newcomer said: "Let him go."

For an instant Carling stood there with the gun under his foot calculating distances, planning moves. But then he dropped his hands and stepped back quietly. He stood there looking hopeless and defeated, a sensible man who knew he didn't stand a chance.

That was how he looked.

But the way he felt was different. He felt more alive than he had for days. He felt as if he had breathed pure oxygen. He felt quick and alert and sure of himself. Once again, he was doing what he did best.

*

Lorenz did not relax. He stayed well back and allowed Zimmermann to put the policeman in a kitchen chair and tie him down with strips of cloth torn from tea towels. Only then did he lower his gun. He was well aware that he was dealing with a professional.

Carling was the only one who spoke. Once he had gathered his wits, he protested constantly: "What is this? Who are you, what do you want?" It was a show of resistance, but it might also be intended as a distraction. Lorenz ignored him. After a while the detective fell silent and sat watching them carefully. He did not appear to be frightened.

Finally, when he was secured and Zimmermann stepped back; Lorenz stood in front of him, looked into his eves and without warning, hit him hard four times across the face alternately with the palm and the back of his hand: One, two, three, four... The man's head jerked from side to side. The grunts which came from the mouth were more from surprise than pain.

The research department of the KGB had worked with Soviet Institute of Psychiatry on interrogation techniques. The experts believed that if a man can endure the first stage, he develops a feeling of pride which helps him over the next. But if he is made to endure pain for no reason at all and is not given any promise that it will stop no matter what he may do, then he is far more likely to take the first opportunity to end it by talking.

For some years now, this had been standard procedure. Lorenz did not particularly like it. It made him feel like a sadist. But one could not expect to enjoy everything one had to do.

He watched Carling's face with professional interest as the detective fought down the urge to panic. He was not ready yet. Lorenz hit him again.

Then the doorbell rang.

For a moment none of them moved. Lorenz snapped: "Who is it?" but Carling only gave an insolent shrug. There were only a limited number of alternatives. It was possible this was a friend come to call, maybe a neighbour worried about the noise...

But more likely the girl had raised the alarm and now the police were arriving to check on their man. Either way the caller could not be ignored. If the door was left unanswered despite the light in the room, it would only arouse suspicion. And if they did answer it, the only way to prove that nothing was wrong was for Carling himself to do the talking.

Lorenz squatted down in front of the detective: "You are going to open the door, " he said. "You are going to say nothing is wrong, but you are not going to allow anyone into the house and nor are you going to try to raise the alarm. "

Carling looked back at him without expression. Lorenz went on: "If you do not co-operate, if you try to be clever or play the hero, I will shoot you in the knees and later I will kill you. Do you understand."

Carling said "yes" a little too readily. There seemed no doubt he saw this as his chance. There would have to be precautions.

While the bell rang a second time and then, impatiently, a third, Zimmermann untied the towels and Lorenz moved the curtain a fraction and looked out into the street. He could not see who was at the door but at least there was no sign of police cars.

He positioned Carling in the hall with Zimmermann in the living room to cover him. He checked that the window catch was free. Then, as the bell rang once more and was followed by frustrated knocking, he said: "Now, open the door."

*

Elizabeth stood between the two men. The Major had been hunting through his wallet for his identity card and the old Admiral pressed impatiently on the bell. It was obvious there was someone in the house but they were taking an awfully long time coming to the door.

The Admiral said: "There's something wrong here. We'd better be ready for trouble."

Elizabeth couldn't believe people really said things like that.

When the door opened there was a man standing well back in the hall who looked at them and said nothing.

The Admiral said: "Inspector Carling?" and the man nodded slowly. The Admiral went on: "My name is Lomas. Royal Navy. This is Major Johnson, Military Intelligence. We have a few questions we'd like to ask you. May we come in?"

Very slowly and with ludicrous deliberation, the man said: "I'm afraid not. It's not convenient." All the time he was making an almost imperceptible gesture with his head as if to beckon them.

The Admiral didn't wait after that. He said: "Come on" and almost ran into the house, knocking the door back on its hinges as he went. The Major was right behind him. Elizabeth put one foot in the hall and then froze.

There was a sudden "phut" like a can of fizzy drink being opened - but rather louder - and the Admiral cried out in surprise and slumped sideways against the wall. Over his shoulder she could see Herr Zimmermann. He had a curious, long-barrelled pistol in his hand. Now he turned it on the young man who had opened the door and fired again. Once more it sounded strange and subdued and now Major Johnson was rushing forward, his hands held out in front of him. Zimmermann couldn't get the gun up in time and the force of the Major's charge slammed him against the banisters.

Elizabeth opened her mouth to scream but at once another man grabbed her from behind. A hand clamped over her mouth jerking her back into his chest. She could feel the fingers pressing into her face. She could feel there was no third finger.

Lorenz.

Over her shoulder he aimed his own gun. She watched it moving delicately left and right as the Major struggled with Zimmermann, gradually beginning to overpower the smaller man. And as she watched, Lorenz moved his finger gently back on the trigger, taking up the first pressure as the Major stayed still for an instant.

He was going to shoot him in the back. Elizabeth tried to shout a warning, but the tiny sound became lost in the confusion. She tried to shake herself free - and at the moment she heaved back against Lorenz, he fired.

When the gun went off, she could see the barrel was pointing too high. The bullet should have imbedded itself in the Major's broad back. Instead it tore through his neck and into Zimmermann's face.

Elizabeth stared at what she had done, her eyes wide above the hand that covered her mouth. She found she couldn't breathe and instinctively shook her head. The hand dropped away, and she was pushed, dazed and shocked, into the house.

*

He had a disaster on his hands. There were bodies all over the hall. Most importantly, the detective was lying whimpering softly and clutching a mass of blood on his shirt front.

Lorenz tried taking his hand away from the girl's mouth. She stood trembling slightly and staring at the mess in front of her. He pushed her into the living room where he could see her and kicked the front door shut. Then he went to Carling. The bullet had passed diagonally across his stomach. The wound looked appalling but would probably not be fatal - not if he was taken to a hospital straight away. Lorenz took out his handkerchief and began to dab at the blood. The detective looked up at him, his face ugly with pain and fear.

Lorenz could not have hoped for a better opportunity. He knelt and began to talk to this wreck of a man. He talked quietly, cradling Carling's head, his lips brushing the man's ear. "It's all right," he said. "We'll call an ambulance. You'll be all right. I know it hurts, but it'll stop soon, believe me. I'll phone for an ambulance. I will, I promise."

Carling looked up at him like a small child who believed everything grown-ups told them. Lorenz said again: "I will, I promise." Then he went on, just as quietly, gently stroking the man's hair: "But I've got to do something first, something very important and you must help me, do you understand? You must help me and then I will call the ambulance and it will take you to the hospital and they'll stop the pain and you'll be all right. But first I've got to find the detonator - you know the detonator, the one for the mine you put on the submarine. You remember the mine, the diver fixed it to the propeller. You had a detonator to set it off by remote control. Tell me where it is and then I'll be able to get an ambulance for you. Just tell me where the detonator is..."

Carling kept trying to swallow and rolled his head from side to side. He was panicking. Lorenz took the opportunity to check the girl. She was still standing there, apparently in shock. She was as safe as if he'd tied her up. He turned back to the detective who was trying to say something. The man's mouth moved, and a tiny dribble of saliva tinged with pink ran down his chin. Lorenz bent towards him to catch the words. But in the end, it was a pointed finger that told him what he needed to know. The man was pointing to the cupboard at the bottom of the bookshelves, beneath the television he had been watching when all this started.

Lorenz should have known it: The detonator was here in the house. Where else would it be? Carling worked directly from Number Ten Downing Street. He had no office where he could leave it, no police station - or course he would bring it home. Lorenz let the man's head fall roughly back onto the floor and crossed quickly to the living room.

*

Elizabeth stood still and allowed Lorenz to walk past her as if she didn't exist. She turned back to the carnage in the hall. She had never seen a dead body before and it seemed somehow unreal.

The detective was looking at her. He lay half under

Zimmermann, his face shiny and grey, clutching at his stomach with both hands. He didn't seem able to speak but his eyes were calling to her it was the most natural thing in the world to go to him. to kneel and touch his face, to murmur some words of comfort.

But as soon as she tried, he looked away. She was puzzled and hurt and then she realised where he was looking: Just out of his reach, still clutched in Zimmermann's hand, was the gun.

Oh God no - not more killing. She tried to calm him and went to move his hands from the huge, gaping wound in his stomach. But he shook his head violently and there was a burbling noise in his throat.

Out of the corner of her eye, she saw Lorenz turn and look at them and then go back to hunting through a cupboard. It was a casual glance, a look that said she could be no threat to him.

Of course: That was the way he thought about her. She supposed that was always the way he had thought about her. But there was something in that look, something that expressed the callous way he had used her, the arrogant certainty that she'd be no trouble because she had played her part - doing anything for the man she loved - just as he and his masters in Moscow had known she would.

And now she was tending the man he had shot and presumably he was confident she would play out that role like a good little girl as well.

She could feel the resentment building up inside her like

a quiet explosion. She found herself thinking, ridiculously, that it wasn't fair. She looked at Carling, almost as if he might agree with her but once again he gestured with his head towards the gun.

She couldn't believe what she was about to do. It was as if some sort of anger drove her on. She tugged the heavy black pistol from the dead man's fingers and waved Carling aside when he raised a red and slippery hand to take it. For once she was going to do something for herself.

Lorenz had his back to her. He was engrossed with a grey box he had taken from the cupboard, carefully examining it as if he was in a shop and wanted to make sure it was all there before he bought it.

Elizabeth raised the gun and held in out in front of her with both hands, pointing it at the centre of his back. She began to press the trigger, but the end of the barrel was moving, she couldn't keep it still. She took a deep breath and held it.

Then Lorenz turned round. It happened so quickly, as if he'd known she was there all along and this was a game and she wasn't allowed to shoot him if he turned round first. He was looking at her, not startled or frightened. Just looking with mild interest as if wondering what the silly girl was up to now. She pulled the trigger. Hard. The gun jerked in her hands and she almost dropped it.

Once again there was the absurd "phut" and then she saw Lorenz flinch. There was a ragged hole in his sleeve and she could see the white of the bone showing through. Suddenly he opened his mouth and roared like a wild animal. And then he rushed her.

She lifted the gun again, but he was across the few yards of carpet before she found the trigger. With one hand he knocked the gun away and grabbed her by the throat, slamming her up against the wall.

For a long time, he just looked at her. He stared into her eyes so that she had to look away. He didn't say anything and then he left her standing there and examined his shattered arm. He made her fetch pieces of the torn-up tea towel to bandage the wound and make a sling.

She did as she was told. Perhaps she had been wrong, and he had been right all along. Perhaps she would always do as she was told and never be any trouble.

She found that she didn't look him in the eye any more - but then again, nor did she cry.

TRIDENT

TWENTY

Channon said: "What do we do now?"

Price said: "Christ, I don't know."

It had been easy enough to decide to follow the others from the hotel - that's what any newsman does when he sees a story driving away from him. But when people start leaping out of front windows brandishing guns, does he sit there recording every detail or does he call the police?

Price knew he wasn't supposed to call the police - not if the whole thing was meant to be a secret.

He said: "We'll give it five minutes."

But it was only three minutes later that Elizabeth Crichton emerged from the front door followed by a man who was only too obviously holding a gun. He was tall and wore a jacket loosely over his shoulders. His left arm was in some sort of makeshift sling. Price was sure it was the same man who had climbed out of the window.

Channon lifted his camera and snatched a dozen frames through the windscreen as the couple crossed the road. "God knows what I'll get with this light," he said. "Who's the guy?"

"That's our man," said Price. "Detective Inspector Carling - must be."

They watched as Elizabeth Crichton stopped at a nondescript estate car and got in from the passenger side. Then she climbed over to the driver's seat as the man got in beside her. The engine started, the lights came on and it pulled away.

Price said: "I'm going to follow them," He reached for the ignition.

Channon stopped him: "What about the others? What about the old boy and the Major. If this guy's carting the girl off at gunpoint, what's he done with them?"

The photographer was right of course. The way Carling had bundled them into the house, anything might have happened. Meanwhile he was fast disappearing down the road.

Price made up his mind: "We'll split up," he said "You check the house. I'll follow these two."

Channon hesitated but he could see the logic. He rooted about in the camera bag at his feet and came out with a small autofocus. He held it up in front of Price's face and said: "Pictures are down to you, Bernie, O.K? Mickey Mouse job - just press the tit. But for Christ's sake get something."

Price nodded. He was watching the estate car turning left at the end of the street. As the photographer got out, he let in the clutch and the door slammed as the car shot forward.

*

The streets were mostly deserted, and Elizabeth drove while Lorenz sat propped against the passenger door, the gun in his good hand. She did as she was told, just as he would expect her to. She said nothing, and she kept her eyes on the road. But she could see, trailing out of his jacket pocket, the wires of the detonator he had taken from the cupboard - and she wasn't staying with him just because he told her to.

Now she was doing a job, just as the Admiral and the Major had been doing a job. She was aware, somewhere at the back of her mind, that she was the one who had made it necessary. But she didn't feel angry or resentful. She just felt very calm and determined - and if only he went on treating her in the same arrogant, self-confident way that he had, then she knew she couldn't fail.

She would have to behave perfectly normally. She wondered how she looked. She was gripping the wheel too tightly. Would he notice that? Would he see the change in her and be on his guard?

Instinctively she began to talk to him. To make the peace as she had done so many times before with some man who insisted on sulking after a row.

She said: "Why me?"

"Hmm?

"When you were looking for a nice gullible girl to bring you secrets, why did you pick me? Did I look particularly gullible?

He didn't reply immediately. Instead he looked carefully at her. She forced herself to relax. She was very good at that.

Lorenz said: "Actually I didn't pick you. You were picked for me."

She grimaced: "What a frightful thought. Didn't you have any say in the matter? What if I'd been 15 stone and with a face like the back of a bus?"

"If you'd been 15 stone and with a face like the back of a bus, then for the first time in my life I would have refused to do my duty for the Motherland."

He chuckled and then added gently: "In other circumstances I wouldn't have seen it as a duty. It's sad that it had to be this way. I don't suppose you'll believe me - but I'm sorry."

"That's all right." She smiled briefly - a little brave smile that never reached her eyes.

They drove in silence for a while, crossing the Thames and heading into Fulham. Presently he spoke again: "You're a remarkable woman, Elizabeth. You tried to kill me - you might have succeeded too - and yet here we are, sitting talking as if nothing had happened."

"Well I didn't manage to did I? That's all there is to it. Like you said. It's over." She changed up a shade too fast and crunched the gears. "Let's just leave it, O.K? I'll drive you to where you want to go and then we'll say goodbye. Don't worry about me. I've been through this sort of thing before ... well, maybe not quite this sort of thing ... but I'll be all right, you'll see."

He said nothing to that and she knew why. She was the only person who knew who he was and what he looked like. He couldn't afford to just say goodbye. She could tell that he was looking at her, wondering how he was going to solve this last of his problems. He was perfectly capable of killing her but strangely the thought no longer frightened her.

Instead she concentrated on taking the car into the Shepherd's Bush roundabout rather faster than was quite wise. She dropped her left hand to check her seat belt. She always wore a seat belt, it was a habit. Lorenz did not. She built up the speed on the wide, gentle curve. The steering became light as the tyres began to lose their grip.

"Steady," said Lorenz.

And then she screamed, locked the brakes and the car slewed diagonally across the road. She heard him shout: "Don't brake!" and then the crash barrier filled the windscreen.

The nearside wing hit first with a harsh thump and Elizabeth jerked hard against her belt, her head snapping forward. And then, almost as if time had slowed down, she watched Lorenz go through the windscreen. He had his hand up in front of his face but because he was already turned towards her, it was his shoulder which hit the glass first. When his head was flung sideways there was no real impact. She caught an image of him in mid-air, his eyes shut and teeth bared, surrounded by a thousand bright shards. He seemed to hang there for an instant, the shattered windscreen suspended around him and then he fell back across the dashboard, gasping from the pain in his arm.

Elizabeth knew it hadn't worked. Even as she released her

seat belt, she knew he was shaken but still conscious. But now she was committed. She grabbed for the gun, getting hold of it with both hands - but she was hampered by the steering wheel and Lorenz was very strong. Even with only one good arm, he could twist the pistol out of her grip.

She launched herself across the seats, partly to get clear of the wheel but mostly to add her weight to the fight. This was a mistake. As soon as she was close enough, with their heads almost touching and the noise of their breathing in each other's ears, he butted her sharply on the bridge of the nose.

She leapt back with a cry of pain and instantly he turned the gun on her. She made a move to towards him. She wasn't going to give up - but then she saw the look on his face. It was the way he had looked at her from the table in the restaurant, mean and cruel and Elizabeth thought: "He's going to kill me. Dear God, he's really going to do it."

In that moment she realised what it is to be absolutely paralysed with fear. She couldn't even breathe. She just stared back at him, waiting for the bullet.

For a second or two neither of them moved. The knuckle of his forefinger was white on the trigger. It needed now only the slightest fraction of a movement - but it never came.

She knew he meant to kill her. She knew he no longer had any choice - and yet he hesitated.

If she ran now he wouldn't shoot. But she knew she couldn't run. That would mean leaving him to get away - to get clean away and take the detonator with him. She was still as trapped as she had ever been.

He said: "Get out of the car."

*

Bernie Price, following the estate car from a discreet distance, had the situation all worked out - and he didn't like any of it.

The detective was whisking the girl away under his very nose and it was entirely possible that by morning he'd have her on a charge under the Official Secrets Act. That meant no story until the trial when everyone would get it - and on top of everything else, Price had never snatched a picture of anyone in his life and he didn't relish the prospect of starting with an armed policeman.

He had that despairing feeling that events were out of control. In fact, he was so preoccupied that when the car in front suddenly turned sideways and rammed the crash barrier, it was all he could do to avoid smashing into it himself.

It occurred to him to stop there and then but that might make it too obvious he'd been tailing then. He carried on round again - that way he could pull up like any passing motorist wondering what he could do to help.

But Shepherd's Bush is a huge roundabout with a piece of common land and a children's playground in the middle. By the time he drew up alongside the wreck, they were both standing at the side of the road. He leaned across to the window: "Anything I can do?"

He gave Elizabeth an encouraging smile, but she didn't seem to recognise him. She was obviously in shock –and then the man bent to look at him.

"Can you give us a lift?"

A lift? Why didn't he just go across the road to the phone box and whistle up another police car? Why not show his warrant card and appeal to the British motorist's natural desire to assist the police? But to ask for a lift...

The man seemed to sense Price's hesitation. He gestured to his car and added: "We'll have to get someone to tow it away but I want to get the lady home first. I don't suppose you're going anywhere near Highgate?"

Price would have taken him anywhere. As it was he said: "I can go via Highgate." He opened the passenger door but they both climbed in behind him. He felt like a chauffeur.

Highgate made sense, of course. A well-to-do suburb in North London with large, secluded houses; it was the sort of place the Special Branch would choose if they wanted to keep someone out of the way - and it wouldn't take Price long to get there.

He glanced at the camera beside him on the seat. He thought of the tactful questions he had for the detective. But if ever there was a moment, this wasn't it.

He drove.

There was only one hope of salvaging something and that was if the girl escaped - the old Admiral had escaped from this sort of custody and he was well past retirement age, so it couldn't be that difficult. He wondered if the girl would try.

He looked at her in the driving mirror. She was sitting against the door - as far from the detective as she could get. She stared straight ahead, unblinking. She didn't look capable of doing anything. He wanted to help her but instantly dismissed the idea. He was just an observer - observe and record, never influence events. That was the rule.

Still, it might help her just to know he was there. As he pulled up at traffic lights, he turned around, smiled at them both and said: "By the way. I'm Bernie Price."

The man said: "Pleased to meet you" but didn't offer his name. The girl turned her head and looked Price full in the face. He wasn't sure whether there was any recognition there and he couldn't afford to wait for it.

He turned back to watch the lights and, desperate to keep the conversation going, said: "Much damage to the car?"

"Bad enough."

This was ridiculous.

*

Elizabeth stared. She couldn't help herself. It occurred to her that Lorenz might notice and become suspicious but there was nothing she could do - she sat transfixed and stared at the man in the driving seat.

Bernie Price. Bernie Price the newspaper reporter; the one who had sat quietly in that ghastly hotel room and given her a whisky and listened to her - and now he was here again, sitting quietly, saying little but so reassuring in his tweed suit and absurd hat that she wanted to weep.

Now she had a chance - together they had a chance. She looked across at Lorenz for the first time since they had got into the car. He was sitting far along the seat, again half turned towards her and with his gun resting on his knee. He had taken the silencer off and it seemed hardly bigger than his hand. His eyes moved constantly from Bernie Price to the road ahead and back to her. She looked away again.

He suspected nothing, she was sure of it. She forced herself to relax, to slump apparently hopelessly in her corner, staring into space. But all the while she was watching and waiting, inwardly hugging to herself the knowledge that two of them, with surprise on their side, must succeed where she alone had failed. All they needed was a chance.

Give us a chance, she thought. Just one chance.

*

Price looked closely at each house they passed. Now they were well into the money belt and climbing Highgate West Hill, it seemed that each one of the imposing Victorian villas could house an undercover Special Branch operation.

But the man in the back let him drive on up the long steep

hill. There were no houses now, just trees on both sides. Price tried to remember when they would emerge in Highgate Village. It was years since he'd been here, not since he'd covered one of those spy scandals at the Soviet Trade Delegation. That was somewhere up here.

He clutched at the steering wheel, not daring to admit what he was thinking: There had been more spies uncovered at the Trade Delegation than ever there were at the Embassy. Was it possible that the man in the back, holding Elizabeth Crichton at gunpoint, was not a British detective at all? Was this the spy, the man Erhardt? And now he wanted to get her into the Trade Delegation where the police could never reach her? For one awful moment Price wondered what it was the Russians wanted from her - and how they might try to get it.

He dragged himself back to the present. This was one time he could intervene. It also crossed his mind that not only did he have a story once more, but this latest development made it better than ever. He told himself that wasn't important. The vital thing now was to stop this man getting her into the building. He changed down to slow the car and give himself time to think.

He looked at Elizabeth in the mirror. He wondered if he could rely on her. Certainly, he could use all the help he could get. But she sat there in the same position, hunched up in her corner and staring into space.

With his left hand, he pulled Dave Channon's little camera across the seat towards him and fumbled for the flash release. There was a tiny click as it popped up. He pulled the camera onto his lap and waited.

They passed the Trade Delegation. Price had to fight off the temptation to slow even more but there was no instruction from the back seat. Perhaps he'd been wrong. They were a hundred metres past the entrance. What the hell was going on?

Then: "The house by the next lamp post. Anywhere here is fine."

He pulled up, set the handbrake and found the shutter button with his finger.

*

Elizabeth thought: This is it. They had stopped at the side of a deserted road. There was a house set back behind a large garden but apart from that, no sign of life.

Lorenz got out and motioned for her to follow. He held his gun low, masked from Bernie Price by the open door. But Bernie was getting out too.

For a moment she thought Lorenz would shoot him. He looked angry and then softened at the last moment: "Thanks very much," he said. "No need for you to get out."

But Bernie did. He was going to shake hands, the perfect Englishman. He had to wish them luck with the car. Lorenz was getting flustered. He had the gun in his right hand. Hurriedly he stuffed it into his pocket.

As he did so there was a blinding white flash. Lorenz

lurched back and Bernie leapt forward, pushing him in the chest.

But even as they went down in the road, the Russian slammed his fist into the little man's face, sending him sprawling, stunned across the tarmac.

Elizabeth was free of the car now. She saw the gun come up and she knew that this time he would shoot. There was no cold-blooded pause while he had to make a decision. This time he was fighting for his life and working on instinct. Even so, she didn't hesitate. Her first stride placed her perfectly and she kicked at his arm with all her might. The gun leapt out of his hand and went clattering right across the road until it hit the opposite kerb.

But the man's reflexes were phenomenal. He swung round and kicked her sharply on the side of the knee. The pain shot up her leg like a knife. She went down, rolling in agony across the tarmac.

She couldn't believe it. There had been two of them, Lorenz was wounded and yet he was still going to get away. She watched with sickening helplessness as he folded himself around like a ballet dancer, put one foot on the ground and pushed himself upright. Then he took two paces to where Bernie Price was struggling to get up and calmly kicked him hard in the stomach.

That was too much. She screamed at him: "You bastard!"

He turned to look at her. It was a look of no more than surprised interest. And then he came towards her.

It was going to go on forever. There was no way out of

this. She looked around desperately, but she knew she didn't have the strength to run.

And then she saw it - lying in the gutter, the streetlamp shining on its dull grey metal: The gun.

Lorenz was still ten paces from her and he paused as she snatched it up.

For an instant their eyes met and for the first time she saw he was afraid. He wasn't angry of calculating or simply an expressionless machine. This time he was actually afraid. He knew that he couldn't hope to cover the distance before she got her finger onto the trigger and he knew that the closer he got to her the better chance she had of hitting him.

Suddenly he spun round and started running, running away from her. For the first time Lorenz Erhardt was running from Elizabeth Crichton. An enormous sense of calm satisfaction welled up inside her as she brought up the gun in both hands, curled her feet underneath her in a kneeling position and took aim.

He ducked and weaved for the first few metres and then he just ran, his legs going like pistons. That was just as well, it meant she didn't have time to think. She aimed at the centre of his back and pulled the trigger.

This time the gun made a sharp numbing bang. She saw Lorenz falter. He took two more strides, but his balance was all wrong. He was running from nothing more than momentum, his shoulders folding backwards and his knees buckling.

By the time he hit the ground she was on her feet. She

could see him moving still. As she came closer she could see the growing dark patch on his jacket, low down and to one side.

She walked up behind him and he got his good arm round under his chin and tried to push himself up but all the strength had gone right out of him. All he could do raise himself up on one elbow. He looked at her then, but she didn't see him. The pleading expression and the open, silent mouth meant nothing to her. She lifted the gun once more and shot him through the heart.

EPILOGUE

Elizabeth had decided early on against taking flowers. She had had enough of men who liked flowers. Instead she brought newspapers - all of them - everything she could find in the station bookstall including the Financial Times and USA Today. Then, on the short walk to the Whittington Hospital, she popped into a convenience store for a bunch of grapes.

Bernie was sitting up in bed looking cheerful. Gone were the tubes and monitors now the internal bleeding had stopped - and he looked a lot better without the ostentatiously large dressing on his forehead.

Immediately he saw her, his face broke into a huge smile. Bernie had a lovely smile, she had decided, and he was completely incapable of controlling it. This had rather surprised her considering how much of his profession involved feigning sympathy so that people felt able to tell him things they shouldn't - and she knew very well how good he was at that.

"Still nothing," she said as she plonked the papers on his lap and placed the grapes carefully on his bedside table.

"There won't be," he said. "George Snelling came to see me last night. There's been a hell of a row about it. The Chairman spiked the story. I had to give him all my notes - he even took the keys to my flat and went round himself. Took the computer. As of today, The Secret Voyage of HMS Vanguard never happened."

She smiled a sad and sympathetic smile: "Your big story..."

He nodded: "Well, not so big now. You've heard the news?"

"No, I came straight here."

"Tattersall's resigned. It was on the Ten O'clock. 'A sudden and serious illness', apparently - no details. Nervous breakdown if you ask me; Earlham's standing in. I've had the leader writer on asking me what this means for the disarmament programme."

Elizabeth was pleased to hear it. At least they still valued his opinions even if they didn't want his story.

"What did you tell him?" she asked.

"Well my guess is that they'll put it on hold while they consult the Service Chiefs. They might even stage talks with the Russians. That's Earlham's style - he's a conciliator."

"Hasn't Mr Narbokov got enough of his plate at the moment - all those riots in East Germany?"

"Well, maybe he'll feel more inclined to see reason."

They fell silent then. Bernie picked up the FT and put it down again.

Elizabeth said: "So what's next for you?"

He seemed glad she had asked: "Well, I've got some sick leave - although there's nothing much wrong with me as long as I don't laugh too much and try and avoid getting kicked in the stomach. I thought I might get away for a bit. Find a bit of sun."

"That'll be nice for you."

"Yes, I thought Greece or Italy perhaps. Bit of culture, good food..."

"I've always wanted to go to Italy..."

"I went to Naples for the earthquake years ago. Wonderful city; always wanted to go back..."

They both paused for another of those silences. Bernie Price, the man who could ask Senior Officers to divulge secrets and sit sympathetically with tearful women until they told him everything he wanted to know, seemed suddenly to be undergoing some sort of internal struggle.

Finally, he said, rather too loudly and too quickly: "I don't suppose you'd like to come with me?"

THE END

AUTHOR'S NOTE
1983

This has been a work of fiction. But while it is easy to say that the characters exist only in the imagination of the author and the reader, there can be nothing imaginary about the British Sovereign. We know who sits on the throne now and we know who will in the future.

But this story would be incomplete if it did not examine the role of the Monarch. No-one is suggesting that what has been described in these pages would or should happen at some time in the future. But as Nevil Shute said when he wrote about the monarchy in his novel In the Wet in 1953: "No man can see into the future, but unless somebody makes a guess from time to time and publishes it to stimulate discussion, it seems to me that we are drifting in the dark, not knowing where we want to go or how to get there."

And he added: "Nobody takes a novelist too seriously. The puppets born of his imagination walk their little stage for our amusement, and if we find their creator is impertinent, his errors of taste do not sway the world."

AUTHOR'S NOTE
2017

Trident was my second novel. The first - best forgotten -

was written in 1973. However, by 1983 I had learned a thing or two about writing. I was a staff reporter on the Daily Mail and I was sent to cover the Women's Peace Camp at Greenham Common. This was a United States Air Force base which the British Government had agreed should be equipped with nuclear-armed cruise missiles.

After all, this was the Cold War. The Iron Curtain still divided Europe.

But there was something remarkable about the Peace Camp. Thousands and thousands of women of all ages and from all backgrounds converged from every corner of the nation to link hands around the perimeter of the base - which was enormous. They camped in the most atrocious conditions, endured the rain and the mud (Peace is Hell, I remember writing). But they wore their woolly hats with pride (woolly minds said their detractors).

To me, there was something impressive and uplifting about them. Remember, this was the 80's - the era of mass-pickets and the miners' strike - pitched battles with the police. A peaceful protest was something extraordinary.

Unsurprisingly, the Daily Mail was not interested in my views. A newspaper's job is to appeal to the opinions of its readers and possibly because I was having to toe the editorial line, I began to wonder "what if..."

And these are the two most powerful words in the novelist's vocabulary. What if this mass movement really took off...

So I went home to my flat in Chiswick and set to work on

my Brother portable typewriter which I had bought in 1969 from W.H.Smith in Sloane Square for £12 19s 6d thinking that now I had everything I needed to be a writer.

My target was 108,000 words because that was the length of Ken Follett's The Eye of the Needle and he had been my role-model ever since I interviewed him over lunch and he ordered a bottle of Dom Perignon and then a bottle of claret that would have cost me a month's expenses.

However, the Laurence Pollinger literary agency would only represent the book if I cut it to 60,000 words - which was probably good advice. They liked the result and on the strength of my new contract, I went out to the River Room at the Savoy and ordered a modest Verve Cliquot.

And that, I'm afraid, was as far as it went. One by one London's publishing houses considered my work and rejected it.

The letters were all very kind and encouraging but no thank you. The book was, said one, just a little far-fetched...

And then 34 years later, along came Jeremy Corbyn.

Nobody believed that Jeremy Corbyn had a hope. Theresa May certainly didn't.

But she and the establishment and the commentators completely misread the public mood in the same way that the people who never actually went to Greenham Common dismissed all those women in their wellies and woolly hats.

What the Greenham women had was commitment. They

had spirit. They had a dream. And in the same way Jeremy Corbyn was able to galvanise the young people of Britain who had never before thought their vote mattered. Until the summer of 2017 who would have imagined that the leader of a political party would be cheered to the echo from the Pyramid Stage at Glastonbury?

I heard about it on the news the next morning - including a report of an interview with the festival organiser Michael Eavis saying that Mr Corbyn expected to be Prime Minister within six months and would scrap Trident as soon as he could.

Later, Corbyn denied he had said it - but then another famous quote comes to mind: "Well, he would, wouldn't he?"

As for me, I was thinking that somewhere in the house I had an unpublished novel which began with just that premise. Come to think of it, the plot also involved a Russian President meddling in other countries' elections. It had an isolationist US President. It had a Royal Family no longer content to smile and wave and let matters take their course...

At least I thought that was what it about. It took a while to find the manuscript - in a tin box with letters from my father to his father and a lot of pictures of unidentified Victorians. But I found it and immediately I sat down and read it for the first time in more than 30 years.

I must say, I thought it was terrific. I can say that because it was written by somebody else - a man of 34 anxious to make a name for himself - and at 68, I am a very different creature.

It did occur to me that I could re-write it ... bring it up to date ... but you have no idea how much damage you can do to a plot just by throwing a mobile phone into it. In 1983 a satellite could not transmit images back to earth. In 1983 there were no personal computers (I was rather proud of inventing the portable version - how did I know it was going to be called a "laptop"?)

So, I left the book almost exactly as it was - just cleaned up the grammar a bit and removed one or two words which we just don't use any more - in 1983 you could say "homosexual" and think nothing of it...

Then I showed it to my son Owen. He had just graduated from the University of East Anglia with a degree in English with Creative Writing. He made two very good suggestions for changes and then proof-read the rest better than I had.

There are probably still one or two typos left over from my local printer running the quarto-sized pages through his scanner and I've left the split-infinitive on the back cover - partly to prove that I'm not yet a pedantic old fusspot but mainly because I don't feel I can bother the online graphic designer with yet another change.

Of course, the biggest difference of all is that I don't have to find another agent - or even a publisher. Self-publishing was once the badge of the failed writer. Not anymore; my old colleague at The Mail, Stephen Leather, regularly publishes his thrillers himself - and why not?

So Trident - the Novel in the Attic - lives again.

I hope you have enjoyed it. I would be thrilled if you were to write a review - and, of course, please tell your friends - especially the ones on Facebook.

After all, the ambition to be a writer is not something that withers with age...

Printed in Great Britain
by Amazon